Meany

by

Peazy Monellon

For my minions, Michael, Morgan and Matty, without whom many things might be possible but none of them worthwhile. You are the reasons I get up in the morning and my smile throughout the day.

Many, many sincere thanks to my friends at Author's Ink, Kris, Anthony, Heather, and Matty for always being there with encouragement and suggestions. And a special thank you to my best brain-storming buddy, Madison. You rock!

CHAPTER ONE:
September, 2011

"I apologize, Father," Eddie said, dabbing at his eyes with the heel of his hand. "Dying is something I've never had to do before and it don't come easy."

The old man looked uncomfortable sitting in that chair. He looked uncomfortable in his skin...fearful even, and as if he was looking for a place to run to.

"I can certainly understand that," Father Murphy answered from his place behind the desk.

Eddie Kingsley didn't look well at all. He was gaunt; clearly his health had been declining for some time. His skin was mottled with hues of gray, eyes deeply sunken in with large, dark patches lying beneath them. And he was sweating profusely although it was chilly in the office. Father Murphy could see that he was in a lot of pain.

"Did you want to make a confession, Mr. Kingsley?"

Eddie chuckled then, but his laughter took on all the qualities of a guitar string that had been turned umpteen notches too tight.

"That's just it," he answered, scratching at his unshaven chin. "I didn't do anything and that's the problem. If I'd have done *something* things might have turned out different. I might have been able to save them kids. This has been eating me alive for years. The doctors want to call it cancer, but I know better."

The Priest leaned forward in his chair. He knew exactly what Eddie was referring to. Southtown was a very small place; not the sort of place where a double homicide goes unnoticed. The details had been sketchy at the time, and the family had remained tight-lipped about the whole thing for all of these years. The priest felt an odd sense of greed almost, and excitement that he was to be the one who finally knew the truth.

"Go on," he encouraged, but the anticipation in his voice was louder than his words somehow and fresh pain flashed across Eddie's face. Father Murphy felt ashamed of his own voyeuristic nature, but this was one fish he did not want to get away.

"Forgive me," he offered. "I only want to help. And I promise that anything you tell me will be kept confidential. Believe me, I know how to keep things between myself and Him." He pointed upwards indicating his Lord and savior.

"That's one of the reasons I came to you," Eddie said. "I figured if anybody could keep a secret... Well, you *have* to, don't you? Whether you want to, or not. You took a vow, right? There's still the family to think of."

"I've kept more than my share of secrets over the years," Father Murphy responded, "and I'll keep this one too, you can be sure of it." This he meant, and it showed.

Comforted, Eddie settled into his chair. He drew one deep breath and began rubbing his head, as though he could reach in and pull out the proper place to begin. He spoke haltingly at first, but as the story progressed it rolled off his tongue as though he'd rehearsed it a million times.

"This is...the real story of what happened to Charles Barnes that night back in '64. You remember him?"

Father Murphy did and he said so.

"People said he disappeared. People love to talk, don't they?"

"They certainly do, Eddie. But he didn't disappear, did he?"

"Nah... He got his comeuppance all right, but he never left that farm. And it wasn't just *two* murders that happened that night, like

4

everyone thought. I was there and I saw what she done. The thing is, I tried to make it wrong in my head and I just couldn't. If the bible says, 'spare the rod and spoil the child', it also says, 'an eye for an eye', and I guess that's right too. Still...what happened ain't exactly right either."

Father Murphy was confused.

"Why don't you start at the beginning, Eddie, so that I can make sense of this?"

Eddie, however, seemed lost in thought. Pursing his lips, he stared out the window momentarily, seeming to consider whether or not he should go on. Father Murphy was relieved when he did.

"People said that he tortured his children with electricity. Later on, I heard them joking that the reason he used electricity instead of burning them with cigarettes, like in the movies, was because he didn't smoke."

Father Murphy was unable to cover the shock he felt at that statement. It must've been written all over his face.

"Eddie? The beginning? Tell me what happened."

"Right. Sorry, Father."

Eddie shifted in his chair again.

"I worked for Charles Barnes," Eddie went on. "I hired on when Charles picked the farm up at an estate sale just before he got married. He got it for a song too. I was fresh out of high school myself and went to live with them straight away. And there was something wrong with the place back then. It just *felt* wrong. It suited Charles to a tee though. I've come to believe that bad energy calls to bad energy and that's probably what was going on there from the beginning.

"He said to me, 'Eddie, my boy, we've hit the God-damned mother-lode!' I remember him clapping me on the back hard enough to send me flying. He was strong, if nothing else.

"We may have hit the mother-lode, I thought to myself, but the mother-lode of *what*?

"Even before the Barnes' moved in there was always a lot of talk around town about that place and I'd heard it all. I grew up in Southtown, just down the road from there. It was a creepy house to begin with. Everyone said it was haunted. It was a couple of hundred years old, for one thing, and a lot of people had lived and died there. But just because the previous owners died, doesn't mean they ever moved out, does it?"

"Well, yes, I suppose," Father Murphy agreed, though not at all sure whether he did or not.

Eddie went on as though he'd forgotten that the Priest was even there.

"Charles married Annette back in 1949, in July, I think. They got married in that little, white Methodist church on the other side of town. You know the one? It was a simple ceremony. Annette wore the dress that her mother handed down to her from her own wedding. She was about the prettiest thing that I've ever seen.

"By four p.m., on the same day, Charles had her in the barn helping with the milking. By a quarter after five, he had already slammed her up against a concrete wall for knocking over a five gallon bucket of milk. I heard her apologizing--said that it was her fault really, and that she should have been more careful. She was as nervous as a long-tailed cat in a room full of rocking chairs! By six thirty, I was already falling in love with her."

It was Father Murphy's turn to shift in his chair. But if he felt a little uncomfortable, Eddie didn't seem to notice.

"Moving in with the family had been against my better judgment. I have to tell you that I was more than a little nervous about that. But I lived in that house for a good many years and never saw nor heard anything I couldn't explain away. Course soon enough the house was

8

filled with children and there was so darned
much going on all of the time, that you wouldn't
have noticed anything if it were there. Now
and then you'd get a feeling is all--just a feeling
that something wasn't right or someone was
watching you. And then the hair would stand
right up on the back of your neck. But like I
said, I didn't actually see anything. Not until
that summer anyways. Not until the summer of
'64..."

CHAPTER TWO:

Summer, 1964

Five-year old Jenny Barnes awoke to the
sound of a commotion. It was not much of a
commotion by Charles Barnes' standards, but
like the early, May morning, he was just getting
warmed up. Her father's voice did have a way
of filling up the wider spaces around him.
Charles was not a tall man. He was of average
height, but stocky, like a bull, his bulging gut
and graying hair telling of his own forty-four
years on the farm. Time passes differently
there. Days are slower, years are longer, and
seasons tend to be hard.

Jenny's day began when Dawny opened
her eyes. Dawn, her four year old sister, was

sleeping in the twin bed next to hers. Dawn was nothing if not lively. Her chubby, round, cheeks were flanked by thick, blonde hair that had never been cut and had grown to almost waist length already. And when her eyes were open, the bright blue fairly jumped out of them and lit up the room. Dawn was the youngest of seven and she was everybody's baby. In fact, she was often called 'the baby'.

Conversely, Jenny was a plain child, dark hair shorn off to above the shoulders, bangs cut too short and hanging crookedly into the bargain. She was more than a bit thin with eyes that were given to a soft grey that spoke of fierce intelligence and determination.

The room around her was plain too, but it suited her. Peeling wallpaper, aging vinyl tiles chipping off of the floor, and a broken, curtain-less window on the far wall of the monstrously large, hundred-year old farmhouse were just part of the landscape. It went like that around here. As she closed her eyes and stretched

11

her biggest stretch, she could feel the warmth of the sunshine streaming through that same window. Could you really call it broken then? It seemed to Jenny that it was doing all that a window should do.

She could hear Daddy yelling in the other room but could not make out his words. Impossible to tell what Daddy was upset about. With all the stealth she could muster, Jenny climbed out of bed, and tip-toed the few steps to Dawn's bed. Placing one thin finger to her lips to signal 'quiet', she put her other hand gently over her sister's mouth. Dawn's eyes flew open, first with sleepy surprise and then wide-awake delight as she saw her sister standing above her.

"Shhh," Jenny whispered and removed her hand.

Dawny smiled.

"We gonna go now?" she whispered. "You promised." Dawn was still not able to pronounce her r's so it sounded more like 'you pwomised'. Jenny loved her smile.

Still dressed in pajamas, Jenny took hold of Dawn's pudgy hand and led her out of the room. They passed into the Spartan dining room and crawled through the legs of a chair and underneath the well-worn, oak dining room table. The table was large. Come dinner time there would be twelve hungry people sitting around it, counting the family itself and the hired men who ate with them. For now though, the chairs were empty and a secret world lay beneath. Crawling was the way they traveled through this room. Always under the table--it was an unwritten rule between the two.

"Are they here today, ya think?" Dawn asked. "The angels?"

"I dunno, let's try it and see," Jenny answered. But she knew they were there. She could feel them.

It would have been hard for anyone else to notice two little girls crouched under that table.

It was a hard and fast Barnes family rule that as soon as a meal was finished, all chairs had to be pushed in until the backs rested against the edge of the table, ready for the next meal.

Jenny reached out, grabbing one chair by the front legs and pushed it until it slid about a foot away from the table. The two waited and watched with the patience of those who know the reward won't be long in coming.

Within the space of a minute, the chair slid itself back into place, seat and front legs back under the table.

"And here they are!" Dawny giggled, clapping her hands. "I love the angels, Jenny, don't you?"

"Let's do it again," Jenny laughed.

For the second time, she reached forward and slid the chair out. Again they waited. This time, however, the chair slid another foot away from the table first, before spinning around in one complete revolution and stopping again for a moment. It then slid back into place under the table.

"Good one!" Jenny cried, giggling even harder now.

"Can we go see the puppies now? Can we, Jenny? Please will you take me now?"

Remaining on all fours, the pair made their way out of their hiding place. As they crawled into the old-fashioned farmhouse kitchen, Jenny was able to make out some of her parent's words. Daddy was talking with Mommy out on the wrap-around porch just off of the kitchen. She could see them now, through the almost floor-to-ceiling windows.

"That bitch! She'll learn to mind her own damned business!"

"Well, what did she want?" Mommy asked. Like Charles, Annette was smaller in stature, but rugged, her own dark hair cut short and interrupted here and there by streaks of gray.

"She wanted to know why Ruth Ann missed school again yesterday. She must be puttin' in some overtime comin' out here on a Saturday."

Mommy was quiet. The two little girls were quiet. Ruthy was expected to get her chores done before she could go to school. If the chores ran long, school was out of the question. There was no arguing that point with Charles Barnes.

"By the Jesus, Annette!" He always said it just like that—by the Jesus--as if Jesus was merely an object. He said it as if Jesus was a noun but not a proper one.

"You get on that goddamned phone and call up the school! You tell 'em we don't need no god-damned school nurse pokin' her nose around here. Christ! I got work to do and I ain't got time to be pissin' around with her."

"So what did you tell her?" Mommy asked.

"Tell her? I didn't *tell* her nothin'." Jenny could see his self-satisfied look through the dusty glass of the lowest pane. "I put the water hose over her head, that's what I told her!"

"Oh, good Lord!" Mommy gasped. It came out almost as a whisper. Jenny could see the flight in her eyes. Annette could take a punch, but given the choice, she'd rather not. "Where is she now, Charles?"

"Hmmph—," he sputtered, "She got in her goddamned, school nurse's car and lit out of here like her school nurse's ass was on fire, that's where she is now!" Charles chuckled. "That'll learn her a thing or two!"

Charles and Annette moved toward the front door and the girls decided to move on. They slipped quickly out the back door just as Charles was really getting warmed up.

"Ruth Ann!" he bellowed. "Get your sorry ass down here right now."

Ruthy, at fifteen, was the eldest child of seven. Charles was proud of that number. For him, seven children represented his sexual prowess. He liked to brag that he was going to

17

keep having babies until he had enough for his own baseball team. They were called, respectively: Ruthy, Callie, Elizabeth, Bonny, Mark, Jenny and Dawn, all ranging from one to two years apart in age.

"By the Jesus! Things are going to change around here, starting right goddamned now!"

It sounded as though Ruthy had better come quickly if she knew what was good for her.

Daddy's voice began to fade as the two little girls skipped across the side yard and headed for the barn. They were free now, at least for a little while. No one would be looking for them before lunch time. The sun was bright and their hopes high. They were going to visit the puppies. There were actually three, grown dogs living on the farm and two of them had delivered litters this spring. Fourteen mixed-breed puppies had arrived on the farm within two weeks of one another. Even now they were snuggling happily together upstairs in the sweet smelling hay mow.

"Will they be waked up yet?" Dawn asked breathlessly.

"Dunno," Jenny answered. "We'll find out when we get there."

It took several minutes to cross the wide expanse of the front yard. The farm, save that it was in such ramshackle condition, was an extraordinary piece of real estate. It was comprised of three hundred and sixty acres of rolling pastureland nestled in a valley, in the midst of the mountainous terrain of Central New York. It was, in fact, one of the largest homesteads around. The family was cash poor, but did not lack for assets. A river ran through the property, though by no means a lazy one. The driving water, hammered through the Barnes' property, bringing life-giving moisture to the crops. It took a great deal of corn and hay to feed the one hundred fifty- plus head of cattle that were housed on the farm. Additionally, there were seven horses, several pigs, chickens, a couple of young sheep in a pen out back, and all of the various barn cats.

As for buildings, the farm didn't lack for those either. There were several large out-buildings and equipment sheds and a massive two story garage behind the house. The barn itself was the size of a small estate with several wings, and those two stories tall. When the wintery weather called for it, all of the cattle could be driven inside. The hay mow was large enough to keep an entire season's hay within. In direct contrast to the condition of the rest of the architecture, the milk-house was spotlessly clean and modern. This was a dairy farm and pipelines carried mass quantities of milk to a huge, stainless steel, bulk tank. Likewise the tractors and other farm equipment were top notch.

As Charles liked to point out, "A job worth doin' is a job worth doin' right, and by the

Jesus, Annette, I can't do the job right without the right tools!" Any money the farm made was quickly spent making the farm better.

The house was also gargantuan, boasting three stories and twenty-five separate rooms. There were seven bedrooms alone in the place and a large apartment upstairs that was currently being used as mother-in-law quarters for Grandma Barnes. It was she who was supposed to be watching out for the little ones while Charles and Annette ran the farm. Grandma was a pious and austere woman though perhaps not very thorough. Most days she could be found sitting in the battered recliner in the downstairs living room, tatting lace. This she did until her eyes bled a milky, white liquid which ran down her cheeks like tears. The strange eye condition was an old affliction, harmless, and one she was well used to. She kept a white, cotton hanky tucked in the sleeve of her sweater with which to wipe the bothersome stuff away.

That was exactly where Grandmother was today when the little girls burst through the sliding doors of the hay mow. Bright sunshine followed them in and illuminated the dusty mow. It was a warm and sweet smelling place. The puppies were wide awake, having just nursed, and were yipping playfully and wrestling with one another in the open center-portion of the building. Peaches, their mother, lay in the hay nearby.

The puppies were somewhat confined to this space as the two large areas flanking it contained hay bales stacked mountainously high.   Stairwells led up to wooden platforms on all sides, by which the uppermost bales could be retrieved.

The instant the puppies saw the girls they rushed to greet them. During the course of the last month, all of the seven children had visited as often as possible given the extensive chore list each was responsible for. They had divided the puppies up between themselves and each of them claimed ownership to two of the energetic creatures. They had of course, all been named and spoiled in turn.

The girls wasted no time jumping into the fray. Throwing themselves belly down into the loose hay, they giggled uncontrollably as fourteen little bodies crawled and jumped all over them, licking their cheeks and nipping at their arms and legs.

Dawn, sitting up now, picked up a spotted puppy and jammed her forefinger into its unsuspecting mouth. "Don't you love when they suck on your fingers?" she asked. "It tickles a lot!" Her face was shining with happiness.

"Yeah," Jenny answered. "They're so cute!"

"I love puppies, don't you?" Dawn asked.

"Yeah. They're just about the nicest things in the whole world." Jenny replied.

"Kitties are nice too."

"Yeah, kitties are nice."

"I wanted the black one that Bethy got."
Dawn often wanted whatever one of the other
children had.

"Dawny, you got the two cutest ones! I
thought Mark was gonna—"

"Shhh!" Dawn commanded. "I'm puttin' him
to sleep." Indeed, she had the wriggling puppy
cradled in her arm, on its back. "Now I lay me,
down to sleep—"

"Dawny! He doesn't like that!"

"Shhh! I pray the lord, his soul to keep. If
he should die—"

The sound of Charles' voice broke the lazy
peace of the hay mow. "Let's go, Girl! Double-
time!"

Jenny and Dawny exchanged horrified
glances. Peaches raised her head and emitted
a low growl. She'd heard this sound in
Charles' voice before.

Dawny set the puppy down on the floor and
began to back away. Jenny looked furiously
around for a place to hide. Spotting the

stairwell to the loft, she grabbed Dawn's hand and ran for it. They managed to climb the short stairwell and duck behind a bale of hay just as Charles burst through the door.

Charles was followed by Ruthy and the other four Barnes children hurried after. Jenny could barely even say 22 Magnum but she knew what one looked like and that was exactly what her Daddy had slung across his arm. In the other hand he held a course, brown burlap bag. Ruthy carried another. Charles leaned the gun against a hay bale.

"Where are you taking them, Daddy?" Ruthy was crying. The other children were crying too. Excited puppies gathered around the family's feet. Peaches was nervously sniffing the shotgun.

"I'm sick and goddamned tired of feeding all these worthless friggin' mutts," Charles yelled. "I'm getting rid of the damned things." He scooped up a puppy and threw it roughly into his sack. "Go on then, help me catch 'em."

"No, Daddy," Ruthy pleaded. "I'll take care of them. I'll get a job somewhere and I'll pay for their food."

"I'll help too," Mark chimed in. Tears ran down the six-year old's face. "I can mow some lawns."

Charles said nothing. Snatching up another puppy he threw it in the bag, on top of the first. Both puppies began whimpering. Charles had wanted sons—big strapping sons to help him work his farm. But while other men's wives delivered labor for the farm, Annette just gave him more mouths to feed.   Four thin girls were born to the Barnes. And then, finally, a son! But this one was as thin and pale as the girls. Thinking that he had the formula though, Charles had increased his reproductive fervor over the next few years, only to be handed two more whining little girls. Well, so much for that plan.

Ruthy dropped her bag and attempted unsuccessfully to grab the other out of Charles' hand.

"No, Daddy. No!" she cried.

"Please, Daddy," the other children chorused. "Don't do it, Daddy! Don't kill the puppies!"

Mark grabbed one puppy and then another, holding them in a near death grip so his father couldn't take them. Callie, Elizabeth and Bonny followed suit. The girls huddled together in a frightened circle, clutching the puppies and each other.

Up in the loft, Jenny and Dawn watched helplessly while puppy after puppy was thrown into their father's bag. For the second time that morning Jenny's hand was pressed firmly over Dawn's mouth. Dawn's tears dripped onto Jenny's hand like raindrops.

"Get some puppies in that bag," Charles shouted at Ruthy.

Ruthy couldn't. Instead she crossed her arms stubbornly and stated, "I ain't gonna do it, Daddy. I ain't gonna—"

Ruthy didn't get to finish her sentence. Charles threw down his bag, prompting a chorus of whelps and whimpers from inside, and slammed the back of his hand across Ruthy's face. Ruthy fell to the floor as the puppies scattered. Her resistance shattered, Ruthy could do no more than lay there and cry. The other children cried harder.

Frightened and confused now, Peaches was running back and forth between Ruthy and Charles, sniffing the bags and whimpering.

"By the Jesus!" he screamed. "You'll do whatever the hell I say you're going to do!" He picked up his bag and began gathering puppies once again. "Now quit your goddamned crying and get up and help me or I swear I'll give you something to cry about!"

Ruthy rose tenuously to a kneeling position. Her sobs quieted now, but the tears still ran.

"Come here, Mr. Black," she sniffled. She gently picked up the puppy that came to her. Cuddling it for just a second, she kissed it on the forehead and placed it in the bag. "Come here, Lil Bit."

Her resignation frightened Mark who, still holding two puppies, ran for the door. Charles was quicker though and was able to catch him by the shirt collar on his way out.

"Little shit!" he hollered, pulling the child backwards and up off his feet. He planted him firmly back on the ground and spun him around. "Give me those sons-a-bitches!" Charles snatched the two puppies from Mark and tossed them into the bag with the rest. Jerking him by the hair and pulling him right up to his face, he shouted, "Goddamnit, Boy! I'll kick your scrawny, little ass, right here and right now!"

The pair was eye-to-eye now, Charles' anger searing hot, his teeth clenched in fury.

Mark, who weighed all of fifty pounds on a good day, was visibly frightened.

"You got a problem doin' what I ask you to this morning? Say?"

"No Daddy."

"Hmmph! That's what I thought!" Charles sneered, shoving the boy to the ground.

It was Mark's turn to be on the floor crying. Charles pointed at the door. "Get your ass back to the house you worthless, little son-of-bitch! Christ! I oughta put you in a home where you belong."

He was referring to a home for 'bad boys', of course--wayward children. It was too much for Mark who jumped to his feet and ran for the house.

Charles looked at the three girls who were still huddled together. "Put... the puppies... in the bag." he said. His voice was tight, strained, and he paused momentarily between the words for emphasis.

The three girls stood frozen, staring at their father.

"NOW!" he yelled.

One by one the girls approached Ruthy. As Ruthy had done they planted a kiss on each of the puppy's heads, whispered a quick "Goodbye, Puppy", and "God bless you, Puppy", and placed them into the bag. When the last puppy was placed inside, they ran too leaving Ruthy alone to help her father finish the task.

Jenny and Dawn remained silent in the loft.

"Let's go," Charles commanded, having gathered them all. Ruthy followed him out the door. Peaches was hard on their heels, alternatively wagging her tail and then growling.

They had been gone mere minutes when the first gunshots rang out. *Pop, pop, pop*—he fired in rapid succession. Jenny and Dawn could hear the puppies yelping. Another crack followed.

"Run you little sons-a-bitches!" Charles shouted gleefully, and fired again. "You can run but there ain't nowhere to hide!"

Pepper, the other mother dog heard the commotion and came running. Jenny heard barking and then growling and then two more shots as the mother dogs were put down. She couldn't listen any longer. Taking Dawn's hand, she descended from the loft and the two began the long walk back to the house.

"Meany!" Dawn said quietly and looked up at Jenny, her tear-streaked face twisted with grief. "Meany..."

Jenny walked on.

At that moment, deep within the bowels of the old house, something stirred.

CHAPTER THREE

Father Murphy was stunned. Apparently Charles Barnes had been brutal as a father. He'd heard many things during his years as the Southtown parish Priest, but this...well, he had no words.

"I don't know if it was the sound of gunfire that woke the dowser man from his long sleep, or not," Eddie continued. "I don't even know exactly when he woke up. As I said before, some of this is speculation. I know I never saw him before that day, but I started seeing him right after. Course, at the time I never knew who he was. All of that came later.

"Maybe it was the sound of all that crying which disturbed his eternal rest in the apple orchard across the road. He had been a part of the farm since the beginning. He'd built the place, for Christ's sake. It was he who had built the small cemetery beneath the Apple trees. You could tell by the dates that his wife and his children had been buried there first. According to the epitaphs, these were Mary Smythe Ten Broek, beloved wife and mother, Emma Mae Ten Broek, loving daughter and Isaiah Jonathon Ten Broek, loving son. The letters on the hand-made headstones were roughly chiseled, as though he'd carved them himself. On both his wife's and his two children's markers, the letters read 'Taken by the Consumption' following their names and dates, all within a few days of one another. 'In the arms of our Lord' was written underneath.

He died soon after. 'Justus Howard Ten Broek' was all that his headstone said. I have no idea who carved his stone.

"Some say he died of a broken heart. People believed in such back then. I couldn't really say. Nor could I really say exactly what woke the dowser man up but I do know that he woke up. He woke up, still dressed in his black, Sunday best, and began walking."

***

The dowser man was sitting in the rocking chair in the corner of Ruthy's room, just to the left side of the closet door. He'd been watching her sleep, though no one could have seen him there. He hadn't been back on this side long enough for that yet.

To be fair, Ruthy had an alarm clock that went off every morning at precisely 4:15am. To be honest, she rarely had the strength to get up at that time. Straight-up if Charles had to go in at 4:35 and drag her ass out of there, she was coming out hard. And that is exactly how he woke her up. He marched right in, snatched a handful of hair from her sleeping head and jerked her straight out of bed and to her feet.

"LET'S GO, YOU LAZY SON OF A BITCH!" he hollered. "TIME'S A WASTIN'!"

Never mind that the weight of her body tore both hair and skin from her scalp, setting a trail of blood on a course down her forehead. Fuck it if she couldn't do what she was told!

"Don't you cry, Girl!" He ordered, "Or by-the-Jesus, I'll give you something to cry about!"

The hateful tears flowed down her cheeks anyway, and she bit her lip as she choked back frustrated sobs.

Charles wouldn't even have to bother with waking the other kids up. Ruthy would go down the line, all the way through Mark, getting them out of bed. The little girls would be allowed to sleep. They were still too young to work on the farm. Ruthy always got it the worst. And since Ruthy got it first, the others needed less convincing. They'd be downstairs within minutes. Charles left as suddenly as he'd come.

***

"It's an ill wind that blows today." Grandma Barnes was saying.

Jenny and Dawn were stretched out on the living room floor in front of her chair, coloring books and crayons spread out before them. Sometimes she got like that. Her face, naturally steely, grew less austere and her voice took on a strange, fleeting quality.

"An ill wind..."

And then just as quickly, she would return to normal. Normal, in Grandma's case meant pretty much silent. It was as if she existed solely to tat the delicate, white lace which grew in ever larger circles as her needles flew with lightning quickness.

The girls could hear Annette on the rotary telephone which hung on the wall, in the kitchen.

"No, John. Nothing wrong. Yeah, just Charles shooting at some rats in the barn."

John would be the neighbor, just to the south of the property. John would be the neighbor who knew darned well how Charles treated his family. John knew, and waited from a safe distance for a full day after hearing all of the gunshots before making the call to determine if everything was all right.

Mr. Simpson knew too. He had seen the bruises and red marks on Ruthy's face all too often. Mr. Simpson was the bus driver who, nearly every morning pulled the bus off to the side of the road to wait for Ruthy, who was invariably a few minutes late. It was against school policy to wait for any student, but Mr. Simpson knew and he did what he could.

Mrs. Caldwell, the school nurse, obviously knew. Yet when asked how her visit had gone she smiled nervously and answered, "It went well. I think that Mr. Barnes will make a sincere attempt at getting Ruth Ann to school on time from now on."

The principal, Mr. Cook, to whom she was speaking, knew. Mr. Cook later commented that the reason Charles Barnes had seven kids was that seven kids could do more work than six kids could. Later, of course, and from a safe distance.

The hired men who lived with the family knew. They knew and they did their best to get the chores done and keep things running smoothly so that the outbursts could be kept at a minimum. They did not, however, interfere with Charles' 'fatherly duties'.

Others knew as well. The world is rife with heroes.

"All right, John. Thanks for calling. Yep! We'll see you by and by."

Annette walked into the dining room and sat at the large table. Her cup of coffee had grown cold while she had been on the phone. She sighed and began drinking it anyway. A large pile of freshly laundered clothes lay on the table next to her sewing machine. These were here for patching. If farm life was hard on people, it was harder on clothing. On the floor beside her, lay a trunk filled with scraps of fabric and used up clothing from which she could tear a zipper or button or make a patch for something that could be salvaged. Annette made all of the children's clothing and most of her own on that old Singer.

She was God-awful weary. Tomorrow was Monday. Weekdays were the hardest. She would be up at 4:30am to help with the milking, which took about 2 hours. Off to work at the grocery store by 8:00am. Back home by 4:30 and straight to the barn for the night's milking. Then dinner had to be prepared for the family and hired men. After dinner she usually went straight to bed, to rest for the following day. Thank God she had the girls to help her out. On weekends she spent her days doing farm chores and nursing the one acre garden that provided whatever food for the family that the dairy and chickens could not. The kids didn't always think that the food was good, but Annette knew that it was good for them.

She had never imagined that life would turn out this way. She'd been young once—pretty, popular and full of hope. When she was seventeen she had fallen in love with a boy named Tommy. Tommy was everything. But Tommy went off to a killing war and never came home. For so many nights she'd cried herself to sleep. And then in the midst of all of that grief Charles had come along. He'd been a handsome young man, with lively, blue eyes. He was the star of his high-school baseball team and looked better than good in a flannel shirt and blue jeans. They'd met at a barn dance and it wasn't long before Charles snatched her shoe and threw it up into the hay mow. That was the shoe that started everything! It seemed like yesterday that Charles brought her here to live on the farm. She had loved the place immediately.

If Annette loved the farm, she loved her children more. She didn't often say that, but not a minute went by that she didn't feel it. It broke her heart to see the way that they were treated every day by their father. She herself had been raised by a spare-the-rod, spoil-the-child kind of father. That had been a part of why she'd married Charles so quickly. It had been just a few months since she'd met him, but she couldn't wait to get out of her own father's house.

The thing that threw her off about Charles was that he was not always mean to the children. Not often, but every now and then, he would buy them something or take a day off and play with them and it would seem like the old Charles was back. During these times she

fancied that she was seeing inside of him—
seeing the real Charles. She'd compose
reasons and excuses for his harsh behavior.
He's worried about money, or he's carrying
around too much responsibility, or maybe he's
just trying to teach the children important
lessons. It was easy to hate Charles when he
was yelling. It was much harder to hate him
when Jenny or Dawn were cuddled up in his
lap while he read the paper or watched the
news. Nearly impossible to hate him when
they came to give him kisses at night before
they lay down to sleep. If there was one thing
she knew for sure it was that her children loved
their father, for good or ill, and they'd miss him
terribly if he was not there. But then he'd get
up the next morning and if something didn't suit
him, another bad day would begin.

She had tried to leave Charles once after
he's slammed her up against a wall and
choked her out for 'undermining his authority'
with his children. There had only been two of

them then. It hurt to remember how hard they'd cried after seeing their mother used like that. She had been prepared back then to move out and take the children with her, but that was not going to happen to the Barnes family. Charles and Grandma Barnes sat her right down and gave her a 'good talking to'. They had let her know that the two of them would stand together in court and swear that she was an unfit mother. She could leave if she wanted to, but not with the kids. Truth or not, those were different times and Annette wasn't willing to take the chance.

Annette Barnes wasn't going anywhere without her kids. So the years passed, the family grew and the lies multiplied. And every night Annette prayed hard that her children could somehow survive this life on the farm. Each morning they woke up just a little bit bigger and a little bit stronger. All of those vegetables were paying off. And she was pretty sure she could outlive that old bitch in the living room! Maybe then--maybe someday...

"Could I have a taste, Mommy?" Dawn climbed up in her mother's lap.

"No, Pumpkin. (She pronounced it *punkin*.) You're too little to have coffee. You wouldn't like it anyway."

"Please?" the child insisted.

"I got your nose," Annette answered, giving Dawny's nose a slight pinch and inserting her thumb between her forefinger and middle finger. The girls loved this game.

"Give it back, Mommy! Please!" Dawn pleaded.

"Oh really? You want it back now, do you? How about if I put it right...here!" Annette began tickling the child, under her arms, on her belly--everywhere. Dawn was giggling madly. Annette flipped her onto her back and quickly pulled her shirt up off of her stomach. Phhhhhffffffffff, she blew great raspberries onto the little, exposed belly. Phhhhffffffff!

"Do me, Mommy! Do me now!" Jenny begged, joining them.

Both girls were so small that Annette easily hoisted Jenny into her lap as well. What ensued was a great, big raspberry fest, with Annette blowing on their stomachs and them alternately blowing on and then kissing her cheeks. There were giggles all around.

All around, that is, save for the recliner in the living room. Grandma Barnes simply elicited an audible sigh. It wasn't much but it clearly said that children shouldn't be coddled in this manner.

Old Bitch! Annette thought, and went on tickling her children.

***

A mile and a half up the road, Charles wheeled his new pick-up truck into the driveway at Bill Monroe's place. He took only a second to admire the well-kept yard and barn before turning off the ignition. He knew Bill was not at home. He'd only just seen him at

46

the auction up town. It looked to Charles like he'd be there for hours. A real stroke of luck! The five, older Barnes children were sitting in the back of the truck.

"C'mon, Kids," he said and walked to the front door. The kids were happy to follow. It was an unexpected treat, stopping by to visit the Monroe's who had four children of their own.

A smiling Mrs. Monroe answered the door, pulling off her apron. Mrs. Monroe kept herself neat as a pin for a farmer's wife. The dress she wore today hugged every substantial curve. The Monroe's were well-off and obviously she wasn't required to work in the barn.

"Charles," she gushed, "How nice to see you!"

"Martha." He tipped his ball cap like a real gentleman. "I thought being Sunday and all, the kids might like to play together a while."

"Well now, I just bet they would!" Martha's smile grew bigger, if that were possible, and she began calling her own children. "Timmy, Cheryl, Olivia, James—"

The four Monroe children rushed into the room and happily offered their hellos.

"James," Mrs. Monroe commanded. "Why don't you grab that football over there and the whole bunch of you go outside and play a while. Mr. Barnes and I have business to discuss."

The unsuspecting children were only too happy to comply as Mrs. Monroe shooed them out the door.

"I'll call you in a bit," she exclaimed happily. "We'll have powdered doughnuts and milk."

Charles smiled too, when she closed the door and threw the lock. *Annette be damned*, he thought. A man had to have something. He could be uptown spending her grocery money on a stupid game of golf. That, he could see her bitchin' about!

***

The dowser man watched and walked, his long gray hair tied neatly back underneath his black hat. He was looking for something and he was sure it was here.

As he walked, he sang an old hymn,

"Bringing in the sheaves

bringing in the sheaves

We shall come rejoicing,

bringing in the sheaves."

For days on end he walked, and as he walked, he did what he did best. He held a divining rod, a kind of forked stick, in front of him, gathering energy and knowledge from the sacred earth beneath him.

"Going forth with weeping,

sowing for the Master," he sang.

49

Many people understood the power of the rod as a means of finding water. He, himself had learned from the Tuscaroras who'd lived around here in those long ago days. He'd been the one to find the water beneath nearly every well dug in these parts back then.

"Though the loss sustained,

our spirit often grieves," the dowser man sang.

"When our weeping's over,

He will bid us welcome."

Few, however, understood the balance of what he gleaned. As he walked, he listened, head cocked, ear toward the ground. For it is Earth, quintessential Mother that she is, who guards the moments and keeps the time. None pass over her without notice and she forgets nothing. She speaks, without prejudice to those who will listen, and the dowser man would, thank you very much!

"We shall come rejoicing,

bringing in the sheaves!"

It was in this manner that the dowser man wandered the property and its buildings. In this manner he discovered the others like himself. Some were hiding in the dampening cellar near the old cistern. He found more in the attic at the top of the stairs. He even met some old friends in the woods beyond. The place was waking up!

It was thus that he began to sense something coming. Something bad...

CHAPTER FOUR

Eddie scratched his head.

"Or maybe I didn't tell that part quite right. Maybe I should just stick to the facts here. I think the truth is that the dowser man did sense something coming, but it was he, who called it. Lest you be thinking that the dowser was our friend, or anybody's friend for that matter, the thing about the dowser is that he had his place and he had his time. He had his loyalties and they no longer lay here. The dowser didn't care who won this battle. He just wanted the place to quiet down! He just wanted to go back to his resting place by the old Apple tree."

Again, Father Murphy wasn't quite sure he was buying the whole story, but as he said, he wasn't there to judge. Instead, he sat quietly and allowed Eddie to go on.

"I know this because I did see him that summer, several times. The first time I watched him walk across the pasture down by the river flats. I knew as soon as I saw him that something wasn't right. First off, his clothes were all wrong for the day. They were too old-fashioned. And the only men who had hair that long back then were hippies and deserters. He sure didn't look like any hippy that I ever saw. And he wasn't quite *there* if you know what I mean. I was just screwing up my courage to say something to him and then he was at the edge of the field and, well...he just vanished! I thought on that one long and hard, I'll tell you. There was only one conclusion though, and I wasn't quite ready to come to it.

"I saw him a couple of more times, just wandering around the place. Then one day—it was the day before Ruthy's birthday-I saw him out behind the barn, in the pasture north of the barnyard. He had the rod in his hands and he was pacing the field. It was hot and I was tired, so I sat for a spell and watched. At one point, the rod dipped hard and he stopped immediately. He looked as though he had struck gold! Dropping to his knees, he commenced to digging with his bare hands. He didn't have to dig too long either. He was good with that rod. Within minutes, water began bubbling up out of that hole and forming a puddle. He dipped both of his hands in the water, scooping up handfuls of the stuff and pouring it down his shirt-front. As he did this, he laughed like a maniac! Then, he stood up and walked right past me, tipping his hat and smiling as he went. I didn't say anything to

54

anybody. Who'd have believed a story like that
one? And it didn't seem like anybody else had
seen him either. They'd have thought I was
crazy."

Father Murphy wondered.

"I checked back an hour or so later and that
puddle had turned into a small pool. Over the
next few days it grew to the size of a small
pond, probably about 150 feet in
circumference, and then it just stopped growing
and stayed put. Charles thought it was just a
spring that had opened up on the property. I
could see him thinking that, since there was
another spring that opened up right into the
cellar of the house. But I know it's that water
that caused all of the trouble with the cattle. I
know it as surely as I know my own name. I
don't know what was in there. I've heard tell
since then that scientists have identified
parasites that animals manage to eat or drink,
which can then drive them to madness just like
Rabies will. I believe that now but I wasn't

thinking about anything like that at the time. Hell, I never even checked it out. I could see from a distance that it was just water. I figured I could save myself a lot of trouble by watering the herd there instead of filling buckets and troughs all day. I wish I hadn't done that now..."

***

The following Saturday afternoon found Jenny and Dawny on a mission. It was to be Ruthy's birthday party that evening. There were many wonderful things on the farm and they knew where to find some of the best of them. Even given that, Jenny worried that her gift would not be enough. She so wanted to see Ruthy happy.

In the kitchen, Annette and the three older girls were making preparations. The smells of Pot Roast and potatoes mingled with that of warm, chocolate cake. Jenny couldn't help licking her lips. It smelled delicious.

"Where are you two headed?" Annette asked, wiping her hands on a dishtowel and tossing it back onto the countertop.

"Just going out to play, Mommy," Jenny answered.

"Okay, then. You two stay away from the barn now, ya hear?" Annette cautioned. The farm could be a dangerous place.

"Okay, Mommy. We'll just stay in the yard." Jenny promised, holding crossed fingers behind her back. The two went out the front door and crossed the porch in a couple of quick leaps. They stopped at the top of the front steps. Bright sunshine warmed their faces and birdsong hurried them along. Jenny bounded down the steps, stopping at the bottom and looking back up at Dawny.

"Ready to jump?" she asked. "Don't worry, I gotcha."

Dawny giggled. "Yeah, just like always."

"One...two...three!" Jenny counted out loud and Dawny jumped.

Jenny caught her just in time. They giggled, having done this a thousand times before. More than sisters, they were friends. Their relationship was like a finely tuned machine, combined energy flowing forward toward a single, perfect result. If one were slow catching on, the other simply waited or helped her along, and always they'd join hands and go together.

"Look what I can do," Dawn announced. Marching back to the steps, she began jumping simultaneously on both feet, back up, one step at a time.

"Anybody could do that, Dawny," Jenny said. "C'mon. We'd better hurry if we're going to go."

Dawn jumped back down the steps and the two headed across the freshly-cut front lawn. Just then Charles' pick-up truck wheeled into the driveway. He and Mark had been off fishing in the river. The girls stopped and waited for their father and brother to get out of the vehicle. Mark got out first and quickly hopped into the truck bed to retrieve the string of slippery catfish they had caught. Charles got out next and looked dubiously at the girls.

"Wanna touch 'em?" Mark teased holding out his catch. Dawny reached out, pulling her hand back at the last second and screwing up her face.

"Eewwww," Dawny exclaimed. "They look sliiiiimey."

"Gonna gitcha!"

Mark began chasing Dawny, holding the smelly string before him. Screaming, Dawn jumped behind Jenny for protection.

"Cut it out, Mark! You're scaring her," Jenny ordered.

"Couple of little babies, that's what you two are," Mark said and huffed off. Dawny peeked out from behind Jenny and stuck her tongue out at her brother's back.

"You ain't right in the head, Brudda!" she said.

Charles watched intently. "What are you two up to today?" he asked.

"Nothin', Daddy," Jenny answered.

"Hmpph," he grumbled. "Must be nice not to have anything to do but piss around all day. Hurry up now, Mark. We've got some chores to do before supper."

"Okay, Daddy," Mark yelled back.

"Must be nice," Charles repeated digging his hands into his pockets. His right pocket jingled with small change and a self-satisfied smile crossed his face as an idea came to him.

"Girls, there's something Daddy needs you to do for him, okay?"

The girls exchanged uncertain glances. What could they do to help their Daddy?

"C'mon now. It'll only take a minute."

Jenny and Dawn followed Charles across the lawn and towards the two-lane, macadam road which shot through their property and wound up the steep hill ahead. The apple orchard waited in the pasture on the other side. Charles looked both ways and seeing nothing coming, he proceeded. He needn't have bothered. There was rarely any traffic on this road. He stopped on the other side and waited for the girls who quickly caught up to him.

"Daddy needs your help for a minute, okay?" Charles repeated. "Daddy needs you to be big girls."

"Okay, Daddy." Jenny felt proud and the light in her face reflected that. "What should we do?" This was something new. A grown-up asking a kid for help!

Reaching back into his pocket Charles retrieved the change, holding it loosely in his palm. He fished out two, shiny dimes and stuffed the rest back where it came from.

Holding out the two dimes he said, "First, let me tell you two girls that if you help Daddy he's going to pay you good. You're gonna make some real money for helpin' me today." Charles smiled warmly.

"I want to help." Dawny said excitedly.

"Me too, Daddy."

"But I said so first," Dawny declared, "so I get to go first!"

"Hold on now," Charles said. "You can both help me and I've got a dime for each of you. That's ten whole cents. Do you know what you can get for ten cents?" His voice was light— playful.

"So what do we gotta do?" Jenny asked. She wasn't thinking about the money. It had not as yet occurred to her what she might do with ten whole cents. She wanted to help her Daddy. She wanted to be a big girl.

Several feet in front of them stood a barbed wire fence. The fence surrounded the apple orchard and the barbs, in part, kept the cattle contained when they were turned out to graze. The fence was only part of the package though, because there was another element to this and all of the fences on the property. Cows are inherently dim-witted animals and at times will wander right through barbed wire, seemingly oblivious to the cuts and scrapes that it can inflict. Sometimes it takes a great deal more to convince a herd that the pasture is where they want to stay.

"You see that fence over there, girls?" Charles asked. "Daddy's afraid the fencer might not be working." Jenny knew that the fencer was what Charles called the metal box which hung on the fence. Jenny also knew that this particular device caused every wire on the fence to give off an electric shock to anything that touched it.

"You girls stay away from that fence," Mommy had often cautioned. "If you don't, you won't soon forget what you get for your trouble." Apparently Daddy hadn't been listening.

"Daddy needs you to touch the fence and make sure the fencer's working." Charles looked intensely at the girls as if measuring them up.

"But we're not supposed to touch the fence." Jenny said nervously. Dawn looked nervous as well.

"Well, I need you to touch it just this one time," Charles answered patiently. "If the fencer isn't working the cows might get out and get hit in the road. You girls wouldn't want that to happen now, would you?"

Jenny thought of the new born calves in the barn. She loved the way the baby hair curled on their foreheads, and how they nuzzled into her face and shoulders when she kissed them there. She thought of how they loved to suck on her fingers and how their faces turned up towards hers when they did so. She did not want the calves to get run over in the road.

Dawn was thinking about the shock that she would receive upon touching the fence.

"No, Daddy. I don't want to do it," she said. Her face grew downcast and tears welled up in her eyes. "Please don't make me do that."

Charles demeanor changed in an instant.

"Well you're going to do it, little Dawny," he sneered. "You're going to march right over there and touch that goddamned fence right now or I'll pop your little ass."

Dawn began whimpering.

"Go on then, before I change my mind about the money and spank you instead."

"I'll do it, Daddy," Jenny said quietly, glancing at her sister.

"Well go on then, I haven't got all day, by the Jesus!"

Jenny began taking the slow, agonizing steps which would eventually bring her to the wire. She walked gingerly, fearing the monster that lay ahead. She had touched this fence before, by accident, and while she'd lived through it, she hadn't forgotten its stinging bite. The fence loomed, electricity promising to jump right out of it at any moment, jolting her with its wrath. An eternity passed as she walked, dreading the inevitable yet wanting the deed to be done. With each step, the earth grew quieter. The sound of Dawn's sobs faded and then disappeared. Even the chattering birds stopped singing and held their breath. All she could hear was the constant, rhythmic pulse of the electric fencer.

Ker –thunk...ker-thunk...ker-thunk... like a heart-beat.

That sound almost certainly indicated that the fencer was in perfect working order. That sound was a feature designed to do just that. Jenny's heart recognized this fact although her brain didn't have that particular knowledge yet.

Ker-thunk...ker-thunk...ker-thunk...come and get me! Ker-thunk...ker-thunk...coming to get you!

She was almost there now. Jenny turned and looked back at her father and Dawn standing there.

"Do it." Charles demanded.

Turning back around Jenny took the final step towards the hateful fence. She hesitated for just a moment and then something occurred to her. She knew what she could do with that dime! With newfound determination she took a deep breath, reached out and touched the wire.

"Yowwwwww!" she screamed, recoiling in shock and pain. She clutched her throbbing fingers and squeezed hard, biting her lip. *Don't you cry*, she thought. *Do not cry.* She wasn't sure why that was important, but it was and she held back the tears. She was no baby. At least that was done and she and Dawn could be on their way. With a look of resolution, Jenny turned around and walked back to where Charles was standing. She said not a word. Instead she met his gaze head-on and with pride, and held out her hand demanding the promised dime.

"All right then," he said.

His voice had an edge to it, as though it weren't all right. Still he gave up the dime and Jenny jammed it into her pocket.

"C'mon, Dawn," Jenny said, grabbing Dawny's hand.

"Whoa! Where do you think you're going? We're not done here yet," Charles said coldly.

Understanding the significance of that statement, Jenny argued, "But I did it, Daddy. The fencer is working just fine."

"Doesn't matter, Jenny. I told her to do something and she's damn well going to do it."

Dawn's tear streaked face contorted with new found agony.

"No, Daddy, please," she begged. "Don't make me do it. It's gonna huurrrt, Daddy."

"Do it." Charles commanded.

"Meany!" Dawny shouted. "I'm telling Mommy on you!"

"You go right ahead and tell your mother, little girl, and then I'll beat your ass and hers too!"

In the end, Dawn's fear of her father won out. As she walked across the road, liquid terror wetted her shorts and streamed down her leg. She didn't so much as turn around and offer Jenny a second glance. Jenny watched helplessly as her little sister's hand reached out, paused and then touched the wire. When Dawny jumped, she jumped, and when Dawny cried out, she cried inside. Dawny, sobbing, raced back across the road and straight to Jenny's side. Charles was looking at Dawn with disgust.

"Awww look at ya," Charles spat. "Peeing your pants like a little baby. You oughta be ashamed. Come on over here then. Now I gotta punish you."

Dawn hesitated for only a moment and then she did come to him, head down in shame and humiliation. He picked her up by one arm and set three, sharp slaps on her bottom. Dawn screamed louder with each slap and tears began to slide down Jenny's face as well. She was a baby then, and no more.

"Now go on to the house and tell your Momma that you need a diaper, for Christ's sake! And you can forget about the ten cents too."

Jenny once again took Dawny's little hand and led her away from this dark game. She walked with her into the house and helped her change her clothes. And then, having done so, took her hand and led her back into the light of the summer day where they could once again play in green, grassy meadows.

"It's okay, Dawny," she said. "Look how far it is from your heart." Truth be told though, this was a wound which not only found the child's heart, but tore straight through it.

CHAPTER FIVE

Ruthy felt like the Queen of England! All of the many members of the Barnes' household sat around the remnants of a fine dinner. Her birthday cake sat on the table before her like a hard-won trophy. The cake consisted of two, delicious layers of chocolatey goodness blanketed in milky, white, butter-cream icing. Sixteen candles dripped multi-colored wax onto the top of the cake. Hank, one of the hired men, had brought along his guitar and was strumming softly while her family sang in her own personal new year. She smiled shyly, sitting at her place at the table.

"C'mon, Ruthy, blow out the candles," Callie said excitedly. "I can't wait till you see what I got you."

Ruthy drew in the largest breath she could and blew a great gasp of it into the hotly burning candles. Her siblings joined in and the tiny flames were quickly extinguished. Laughing, Annette began cutting huge chunks of chocolate cake and loading them onto dessert plates, heaped with vanilla ice cream. Ruthy got the first and biggest piece. Her face shone with happiness as she began shoveling the cake in her mouth. Charles turned his attention to his hired men and they moved to the living room to discuss the following day's chore list.

"Open your presents, Ruthy. C'mon." Callie pleaded.

Several packages wrapped in tissue-paper were lined up in front of Ruthy. She stopped eating and tore into the first package. Inside was a beautiful and delicate lace tablecloth from Grandma Barnes.

"For your hope chest," Grandma said absently.

From his place in the corner of the dining room, the dowser sensed something about Grandma Barnes. His curiosity peaked and he decided an experiment was in order. His face tensed just a bit as he focused.

"The river is mighty high this year," Grandma said, and then looked confused. She turned her head and looked in the direction of the dowser, as if she knew where the errant thought came from. The dowser stood very still and waited.

"Thanks, Gram," Ruthy answered, ignoring the inconsistency. "I'll treasure it." Ruthy couldn't even imagine being married, let alone

laying out a dinner which required such finery.
All of that seemed a long way away.

"Open ours next," Callie teased.

Elizabeth and Bonny smiled smugly. The
three girls had saved their money and gone in
together to pay for Ruthy's gift. Ruthy grabbed
the package which was marked 'Love, Mommy
and Daddy'.

"Ya mean this one?" she asked. There
were groans all around. Upon opening it, she
found a beautiful, aqua colored, silky dress
inside. The dress was formal, tea-length with
slender straps and a beautiful bow carefully
hand-stitched into the waistline. She knew her
mother had to have spent many hours creating
something so fine. She had never had a dress
like this and she carefully folded its creamy,
blue-green softness, placing it back in its box.

"Thank you, Mom." She said and stood and
hugged her mother. "I can't wait to wear it."

"You're welcome, Kiddo," Annette
answered. "I figured it's probably about time

you were allowed to go to some dances at the school. I always loved that when I was younger."

"You mean it, Mom?" Ruthy gushed.

"Sure do. You're growing right up, Ruthy. You're old enough to date now."

Ruthy blushed. The sisters could wait no more. "C'mon, Ruthy! Open our present now!"

Ruth began to tear at the paper which concealed her sisters' gift.

"Be careful!" Elizabeth warned. "It's breakable."

Inside was a new 45 rpm record. The song was recorded by a group called The Temptations and happened to be Ruthy's favorite new song, My Girl.

"Wow, this is great!" she exclaimed.

Mark was standing behind Ruthy in order to look over her shoulders. "Hey!" he said, "I know that song!"

Callie, Elizabeth and Bonny beamed. Mark picked up a dinner knife, holding it like a microphone, got down on one knee in front of Ruthy and began to sing. He sang rather loudly, although he did have a fine voice.

"*I've got sunshiiiiine...on a cloudddy daaaaaaaaay.*"

Ruthy grinned. "Aren't you something, Mark!"

"*When it's cold outsiiiiiide, I've got the month of Maaaay.*"

Ruthy beamed.

"*Well, I guess, you'll say—*"

"ANNETTE!" Charles shouted from the next room. "A little peace and quiet here, if you don't mind? I can't hear myself think!"

"Shhhhh," Annette cautioned Mark, who had already stopped singing. "Daddy's talking business. Let's just open some more presents, okay?"

"Now mine," said Mark. "It ain't much but it's all I knew how to do."

Mark's gift was a wooden plaque he had made himself using Charles' tools in the garage. He had carved Ruthy's name into the front.

"It's really nice, Mark. Thank you. I'll put it on my dresser."

"I got you something too," Dawny broke in. She got up, raced into her bedroom for a split second and returned grinning, with both hands concealed behind her back.

"I got you two presents, and here's one of 'em!" One little hand emerged from behind the back and in it was nestled a pint-sized bunch of honeysuckle. The Barnes children loved to pick honeysuckle which grew wild about the place. At the base of the brilliant, orange and yellow flower was a tiny nodule filled with sweet nectar. It was a real treat to bite the nodule and let the syrupy, sweet stuff ooze across their tongues.

"Mmmm," Ruthy said. "Now that's a tasty present!"

Dawny giggled and presented the other hand. In it was another bunch of flowers--

Impatiens this time. These were an old favorite for the Barnes children as well. It wasn't the pretty, red-orange blooms which attracted them however. Impatiens bear a seed pod, about a half inch long and shaped like a tear drop. The slightest touch causes them to burst open, like popcorn popping, and toss their seeds to the wind. The children loved to pop open the pods, which tickled their hands and then curled in upon themselves.

"Poppies!" Ruthy exclaimed. "You got me some poppies!" Even at sixteen she still loved the little pods.

"Those are Impatiens," Annette corrected her. "Or some people call them Snapweed."

"No, Mommy," Dawn said with certainty. "They're poppies, all right! Just try one and you can see. "

The dowser smiled. He was warming up to this family.

"Have you girls been out by the road again?" Annette asked. "Seems to me that those mostly grow way up the hill, beside the road." Her face said that she was not very happy about that.

Dawn and Jenny looked at one another a bit nervously. Earlier, they'd been worried that they might be caught during the act, but it had never occurred to them that they could be caught after it.

"No, Mommy," they lied. Annette didn't fail to notice the fingers crossed behind their backs.

"You wouldn't lie to me now, would you?"

"No. Mommy."

"Because you remember the story we read? About Pinocchio? Remember what happened to him when he lied?" Annette questioned. "You wouldn't want that to happen to you, would you?"

Jenny knew better. Dawny, however, immediately smashed the palm of her hand against her nose to guard against the inevitable growth.

"No, Mommy. I promise." Tears filled her eyes, but she stuck to her story. "We didn't go out of the yard." The little hand remained on the nose, while the rest of the family sniggered.

"Well, maybe we'll talk about this some more tomorrow," Annette answered. "You can't run around lying all of the time." Dawny stopped crying and looked relieved.

"Now my present," Jenny announced as she handed Ruthy a tiny package. The wrapping paper was a page torn from her coloring book.

"Hmmm," Ruthy wondered. "What could be in here? They say the smallest packages are always the best."

At first, it didn't look like there was going to be anything at all inside, but then Ruthy found the prize. Wrapped in the paper was one, thin dime, even shinier now that Jenny had spent a good portion of the afternoon polishing it. Ruthy looked confused at first and then the realization hit her like a tank and she knew exactly how her sister had gotten the money.

She recalled, with horror, her own excursions to 'test the fence'. Emotion overwhelmed her. Ruthy stood straight up, clutched her stomach and threw up in her cake.

"What the—? Oh my God, Ruthy!" Annette cried. "What in the world's the matter?"

But Ruthy was on her way out the door.

Annette might have gone after her if it weren't for the fact that Jenny was now crying.

"I didn't mean it, Mommy. I just wanted to give her a gooood present. Why'd she do that, Mommy? Why didn't she like my present?"

Dawny, seeing her sister's tears, began to howl. "I don't like birthdays, Mommy. My nose feels fuuuunny."

Everyone else sat in mute shock. From the living room Charles shouted, "Jesus Christ, Annette! What the hell is the matter with them kids? Shut 'em the hell up! We're trying to talk business in here."

And just that quick, the party was over.

"The ones in the attic are not nice," Grandma Barnes said to no one. "Not nice at all…"

***

Rage welled up inside Ruthy as she ran across the darkened yard. The angrier she became, the faster she ran. Her feet knew every step of the way and without thinking she crossed the back yard and burst through the doors of the horse barn behind the house. This was where she came when she needed to be alone. It was where she came to fight the good fight inside of her head. The horses understood. They were on her side and they'd listen to her problems for just as long as she needed them to. But even the horses weren't always enough. She fought, unsuccessfully to hold back the sobs that wracked her chest.

She turned her back toward the horses, and fumbled along the wall with her left hand until she found the light switch. Immediately she saw what she was after. Reaching up, she grabbed the piece of broken glass that she kept stowed on a beam above the light switch. Pulling up the hem of her shorts, she began to dig the glass into her tender thigh. As the first drops of blood began to paint their way along the familiar trail on her leg, Ruthy gave in to her anguish.

Suddenly, from behind, a hand reached out and grabbed her by the wrist.

"Not again, Ruthy," an angry voice commanded.

Ruthy's sobs froze and she shrieked as she rounded upon the dark haired, young man that had been standing in the darkness.

"Gimme the goddamned glass."

"Adam!"

Adam Morris lived on a neighboring farm nearly two miles away and he and Ruthy had been the best of friends since they met on the bus the first day of kindergarten. More recently however, their relationship had grown up.

"Christ, Ruthy, what're you doing? I thought we were done with all this. That Son-of-a-bitch! What's he done now?"

Adam took the glass away from her, and tossed it angrily into a nearby trash barrel. Ripping the bandanna off from his head, he kneeled down and began swabbing the blood from her thigh. Applying pressure with the bandanna, he worked to stop the bleeding with one hand, wrapping his free arm around her. He let her cry into his chest for a while.

"Why you cryin', Baby?" he asked, stroking her hair.

"I'm not crying, you jerk! You scared me is all. What are you doing here?"

"Waiting for you, don't you remember? You were supposed to meet me here an hour ago. I fell asleep waiting. And yes, you are crying. What's he done now?"

"Oh, Adam," Ruthy sobbed, "I just can't believe it. There's never been a bigger son-of-a-bitch born on the face of this Earth! He's started on the little kids now. He's got Jenny and Dawny touching the electric fences for dimes. Look. Jenny gave me this for my birthday." Ruthy opened her clenched fist to reveal the dime. Adam groaned as he took it from her.

"Why does he do that?" he wondered aloud. "It's so damned mean. What'd your Ma say?"

"Ummmm...she didn't exactly make the connection. She's working all the time and she's so tired she doesn't seem to see anything anymore."

Adam sighed. "Look, Ruthy, this has got to stop. I can't stand seeing you this way. Every morning on the bus when we're pulling in to pick you up, I'm holding my breath. I'm holding my breath, for God's sake, and praying that I don't see another black eye, or worse. I'm sitting there praying that you even make it on the bus, or through another day, for that matter. And now that school's over for the year... One of these days, he's going to kill someone and I couldn't stand it if it was you."

"What do you want me to do, Adam? He's my father. What else can I do?"

Adam hugged her and kissed her forehead.

"Don't cry, Ruthy. We'll figure it out. I'm gonna take care of you, okay?"

"You? What are you gonna do about it?"

"Well...you remember I told you I wanted to talk to you tonight? Come here and sit down."
He took her by the hand and led her back into his corner where they sat down in the hay.
"I've got a plan, Ruthy, and I think it'll work."

"I'm listening."

"I want you to run away with me," he began, his dark eyes earnest.

"What? Adam, that's crazy talk!"

"No, it isn't. Think about it. I graduate in a couple of weeks. I'm done with school now. I love you, Ruthy. I want to marry you."

"Marry me?" Ruthy gasped. "Have you gone straight off the deep end? I'm sixteen years old today."

"Yeah, but this is different. We can't wait any longer, Ruthy. We've got to get you out of here, and soon. Besides, my mother got married at fifteen and she did just fine. You do love me, don't you?"

"Married?" Ruthy still could not believe what she was hearing. "Run away?"

"Well, I don't mean today," Adam said, "but soon. I've got a plan. Wait till you hear!"

"But I have two more years of school. How am I going to run away with you and still finish? And what about my sisters and my brother? What about my mother?"

"Look, Ruthy. I can't do anything about your family, but I can sure as hell get you out of here. I'll be eighteen at the end of the summer. I'll be old enough then to take care of you. I'll be able to get a real job and you can finish high school wherever we go. You can pick wherever you want. Where do you want to go, Baby? Pick anywhere you like." He stood up and smiled. Bowing deeply he said, "Your wish is my command!"

Ruthy couldn't help smiling at that. She stood and met his gaze.

"What will we do for money until then?" she asked.

"That's the best part! I got me a summer job and I'm going to save every dime." As if to prove that, he held up Ruthy's birthday dime and winked. "We'll start with this one."

"I don't know, Adam, if my father catches us—"

"Yeah," he answered glumly. "If he catches us, he'll kill us. Just have to make sure that doesn't happen then. We have to be really careful. Choose somewhere far away, Ruthy, somewhere he'll never find us."

"I always wanted to go to California. Can we save enough money to get to California?"

"Done!" Adam exclaimed. "And that's the beautiful part--the job I got? It's working for your father, Ruthy! Not only will I be here every day to make sure he doesn't hurt you, but it'll be his money that pays our way to California!"

"Here? You're working here? And you'll be here every day?" Ruthy asked throwing her arms around his neck. "Oh my gosh! I can't wait till you start!"

"You do love me then?"

"You know I do," she answered. "But for now, I'd best be getting back. They'll be looking for me."

"Yeah, probably right. Can I walk you?"

"No. You'd better not. I'm okay, really."

"Okay. Well, I'll go then. Dry those tears, Girl," he said as he brushed his hand across her cheek. "See ya tomorrow, Baby." Adam took her face in his hands and kissed her, first on the lips and then again on the forehead. "Bright and early."

And just like that he stepped out the door and disappeared into the shadows. Ruthy began walking toward the house. She hadn't gone more than a few steps when she sensed something.

The dowser was walking right beside her, though she could not see him in the darkness. If she could have seen the wicked, toothy grin on his face she probably would have fainted. He was playing a game with her, stepping at the exact moment she took a step, walking a few steps ahead of her and then falling behind, and finally falling back into rank with her.

"I know you're there," she said quietly.

Had she been able to see him, she would have first witnessed shocked surprise upon his face, and then delight.

"Get away from me, God damn you," she hissed.

The dowser would do as she asked. But first, he sped up just enough to place himself directly in front of her. Stopping now, he simply grinned and waited for her to walk right through him. Abruptly, Ruthy felt the extreme cold and the hairs on the back of her neck stood straight up. Her arms and legs tingled with chill bumps. It lasted for a mere second and then Ruthy was running once more for the house.

CHAPTER SIX

Father Murphy excused himself and went to make a phone call. The meeting with the vicar would have to wait until tomorrow. He had a feeling that Eddie was just getting warmed up. Moments later, he returned.

"Go on, Eddie. I have all day now."

"I appreciate that, Father. Lord knows I do... Now where was I? Oh yeah, I remember."

He took a deep breath and prepared to go on.

"Now If I'd have known what went on in the basement that day after Ruthy's birthday party I may have put some things together. Lord knows the signs were all around me. I just couldn't see it. I guess you could say that I didn't want to see what was happening. I don't know about that, but I was blind to it, that's for sure. It was right about that time that I noticed something strange about the house. I was heading out of the barn, and up towards the house one evening. I was looking right at the house, thinking what a beautiful, old place it was. And you may not believe this next part, but it's true. I didn't believe it myself at first, and that was the problem. Anyways, I was looking straight at the house and I swear I heard the faintest *click* inside of my head. And right then the house just froze in time, like a snapshot. Only something changed. On the far left side of what I saw, the color looked like it had drained right out of the thing! You could almost see a crease in that photo image of the place and everything on the left side of that crease showed up in black and white! See what I mean? I blinked once, and everything looked normal again. I told myself then and there, *Eddie, you have been working way too hard. Now you've gone and imagined something that ain't no way possible.* And that's the last I thought of it for a few days."

At this, Father Murphy raised his eyebrows in disbelief. Eddie never noticed.

"I'll tell you something else, if I'd have known what went on down in that cellar, I'd not have rested easy until I got Annette and those kids out of there. Just the thought of little Jenny down there alone drives me nuts! Now, you may be wondering why I stayed on that farm so long, what with Charles being such an ass and all. But don't you see? That's exactly why I did stay. I stayed and did what I could to make things easier on them. Annette and the kids, I mean. I loved each and every one of those kids like they were my own. And

Annette...well, I never did her any dishonor, though I thought the sun rose and set by her. I just stuck around and helped wherever I could."

***

If there were anything resembling a cool breeze on the farm today, Jenny couldn't find it. The sun was high in the sky and hot as she rounded the house into the back yard. The humidity in the air was almost tangible and it lay on her like the heavy feeling of Ruthy's party the night before. *Why did Ruthy act like that?* She wondered. *What did I do wrong?* Sometimes grown-ups were so confusing and Jenny had the sense that her sister was crossing some sort of invisible threshold into that other, adult dimension. It troubled her to no end that Ruthy was slipping away from her.

She had already wandered a good, long way in the hour or so that Dawn had been napping inside. Her sweaty clothing stuck to her uncomfortably and she scratched at the heat rash that had begun to develop on her stomach and chest. Shading her eyes against the sun, she made for the sheep pen. She loved the gentle, thick-haired lambs. Maybe they could help her sort it all out.

Maybe Ruthy was just tired, like Mommy sometimes got to be. Sometimes Mommy cried when she thought no one was looking. Jenny hoped Ruthy wasn't going to start that business. Maybe she could help her a bit more--do some of her chores or something.

Jenny's peripheral vision caught something amiss just at the edge of the house. The cellar doors lay open. These were two, heavy wooden doors that were set in framework nearly parallel to the earth and were generally locked against the children. They were never to play down there. *I wonder who's down there*? she thought, as she wandered over to the steps.

The stone steps were blessedly cool on her bare feet and she stepped gingerly into the dimly lit cellar. Several windows set into the walls just above ground level allowed beams of sunshine to funnel in. It took only a moment for her eyes to adjust and she could see surprisingly well considering the dim nature of the space.

"Hello?" she called to no one. "Anybody down here?"

The cool atmosphere combined with the happy chance of finding herself alone in this forbidden place and distracted her from her worrisome mood. This was the belly of the house, but in truth, there wasn't a lot to see down here. It was far too damp to store anything of value. The floors were nothing but the dirt that had been there for centuries. Rugged stone walls and heavy, wooden beams throughout were the skeleton that supported the structure above.

"*Welcome*," those walls seemed to whisper. "*Come on in*."

On her right, the oily, mechanical monstrosity that was the coal burning furnace lay sleeping. Next to that were three very large, wooden coal bins that were nearly empty now. Bits of coal that had fallen out of Daddy's shovel on the way to the furnace littered the floor.

"*No need to worry*," the walls said. "*No one will know you're down here*."

On the far wall, next to a workbench, was a five-tiered shelf which was half filled with jars of canned goods, grown dusty now. Soon, those shelves would be filled to over-flowing with vegetables from Mommy's garden. Jenny wasn't interested in that though. She walked deeper into the cellar and around a stone partition towards the left and front of the house. It was a bit darker this far in and she squinted in an attempt to see the small pool of water in the floor. She knew it was here somewhere—

had seen it once when she came down to help Mommy carry bottles upstairs. From nowhere a tiny breeze lilted in and blew her hair into her face. Just as quickly it subsided and she shivered as she wrapped her arms around herself.

There! she thought as she spotted it. And there, in the floor was the icy pool of water she had been looking for. The water was black and still and she searched fruitlessly for any sign of a bottom. Mommy called it a spring and said the water came from deep under the ground. In olden times, this was where they got the water from. They didn't have pipes and faucets to bring the water into the house like now. A stone ledge, about a foot and a half wide framed the pool. She wasn't allowed anywhere near that ledge. Built into the wall, just on the other side of the spring was a stone niche perfect for sitting in.

"*It's okay,*" the walls seemed to say. "*Sit a spell and cool off. No one's watching.*"

The rock was well-worn, as if sitting were something that had happened a lot down here. Jenny sat back, leaning into the wall and closed her eyes. The cool quiet of the cellar felt wonderful. This was a whole different world than the one above, and she grew sleepy as another gentle puff of air caressed her face, lulling her--willing her to drift off. She'd had little sleep last night.

And as she drifted off, the image of another child crept into her world. A young girl, about twelve-years old, sat in this very spot. It was as if Jenny was standing next to her, and looking on, though the image was hazy. The girl, whose long blonde hair was tied up in a ribbon and hanging in ringlets, was reading from a leather bound book. No! That wasn't right at all. She was writing in it with a feather! A bottle of dark liquid and a beautifully carved wooden box rested on a small, roughly hewn, wooden table next to the niche. Beside the ink, a candle burned, illuminating the girl's face.

How beautiful she looked in her white, eyelet lace dress! With her soft countenance and quiet manner, she looked to Jenny like a princess Mommy had once read to her about, or like an angel. She turned her face toward Jenny and smiled.

"Oh! Hello there," the princess offered. Her voice sounded almost hollow, as if it came from far away and all around, and it echoed slightly as it bounced off the stone walls. "Gracious! You've finally made it then. I've been waiting ever so long for you! My name is Emma. Emma Mae Ten Broek."

Emma held out her hand as if to shake.

"My name is Jenny—Jenny Lee Barnes."

Reaching out, she took hold of Emma's hand. For an instant, she felt an enormous pulling sensation. She instinctively yanked back her hand and arm, but felt herself propelled toward Emma's side anyway. It was a very short distance, but felt like swimming through gelatin.

"Oh, that's better," Emma said. Her voice sounded more normal now.

"I live here," Jenny said.

"Yes, I know. I lived here once too," the princess said. A strange longing colored her face as her words faded into nothing. "I like it down here." She lay the pen down and blew gently on the page before her.

"Me too," said Jenny.

"It is so noisy upstairs!" Emma responded. "Goodness! With all of the hustle and bustle, sometimes I can barely hear myself think!"

"Mmmmm...I know what you mean."

"This is my favorite place to be alone," Emma said. "I come here a lot. I love to sit and smell the herbs and roots Mamma has drying down here. Can you smell them?" She pointed to the beams over her head.

Jenny looked upward and saw tiny bunches of dried flowers and herbs hanging on strings from the rafters above. And she *could* smell them! The scent was dry and sweet and she could see other things now—things that were not there moments ago. There were bins of potatoes and strange looking roots sitting nearby. Several large crocks were lined up against the wall.

"We kept it open in the summertime so that it was dry down here, not damp like it is now," Emma said. "It's been ever so long since I've been here. Have you seen my Papa?"

"I don't think so," Jenny answered. "I don't know who he is."

"You're very young, aren't you?"

"I'm five," Jenny answered. "Five and a half, but Mommy says I'm very smart for my age."

"Yes, I thought so," Emma said. "You're about the age my brother was. We were beset by the consumption."

"Consumption? What's consumption?"

"It's of no matter now," Emma answered. "And I don't like thinking of it. Would you like to know a secret instead?"

"Sometimes my sisters tell me secrets," Jenny said thoughtfully. "I mostly like them."

Emma sprang lightly up and out of the niche. Smoothing the wrinkles out of her dress, she said, "I'm very pleased to meet you, Jenny. It's good to have a friend again. I just know we're going to have such fun together!" Once again she held out her hand.

Jenny smiled and shook hands. Emma tucked the book, ink well and pen neatly into the little, wooden chest and gathered up the candle.

"Come with me then," Emma said and began to walk away. Jenny hesitated for a moment. "It's all right, Silly, I have the candle. You needn't be afraid of the dark. Papa likes to say there's nothing in the dark that's not there in the light."

And suddenly Jenny noticed just how dark it had grown in the basement. It was as if night had fallen.

"You needn't fret," Emma said smiling. "I'll see you back safely."

Turning, she led Jenny around a corner and through an open doorway, into a small stone enclosure near the niche. It was totally black in here save where the candle lighted the way. The room contained more shelves, again filled with roots and dried blooms on one side. On the other side, a stack of dusty, dark brown glass bottles were stacked in a loose pyramid. Jenny studied the tops of the bottles which were corked and sealed with wax.

"What's in these?" she asked.

"Oh, that's Mama's famous Dandelion wine," Emma explained. "She makes it herself. Papa gives it as gifts on the Yule. And oftentimes he offers it up to guests 'round the fireplace on a wintery evening. Papa lets me have just the teensiest sip from his cup sometimes, though women are generally forbidden to imbibe. It warms your throat first, and then your tummy. Mama says they ought to let women have it. She says that it would cure Hysteria and the Vapors. Chief Hadawa'ko calls it firewater!"

"Chief Hadawa'ko?"

"Yes, yes! I know! Many people think it's un-Godly to allow savages into your house, but Papa says that Chief Hadawa'ko is more civilized than many in this rough country. Papa was educated in one of the finest academies in Massachusetts. He knows just about everything!"

"Massachusetts?"

Emma laughed and the sound carried as lightly as musical notes through the air.

"That's okay," she said. "I'll teach you all about it. I can teach you lots of things. Papa taught me my letters, though Mama said that was a wicked thing to do. Women aren't allowed to attend the Academy, but Papa says a proper girl should have something of an education. He says that I am too smart to be tied to needlepoint for my entire life."

Turning away from the wine, Emma pointed in the direction of the back wall.

"There's a secret hiding place in here," she said. "Papa cut it into the stone for me when I needed a place to hide my journal. Papa is such fun. He plays the fiddle, you know. And he dances like such while he does so…"

Emma set the candle and the box down on a shelf near the back of the small room. Bringing her arms up to nearly shoulder height, she curled them in on herself and began playing an invisible fiddle. As she did so, she whirled around the small space, sometimes gently leaping and sometimes tapping her slipper-clad toes on the dirt floor. Jenny could hear the music now, and she visualized Emma's father dancing in a black suit with his graying hair tied back.

"See?" Emma asked. "He dances like this."

"Yes, I do see," she answered.

"It was such fun back then! I truly enjoyed living here." Emma said. "But that was long ago, and we must speak of other things. I cannot be sure of how much time we may have."

Reaching up with both hands she took hold of a rock in the wall and deftly freed it from its stony prison. An empty space slightly larger than the box itself was revealed. She set the rock down beside the candle.

"Papa's very clever at making things," Emma explained. "He made me this hiding place. He made the book that you saw me writing in too."

"I know how to write," Jenny said. "I learned all of my letters in school this year. I can write my whole name now."

"Do you have a journal, then? Like mine?"

"No. I would like one very much though."

"I see," Emma answered. "Well, if you don't mind having one that's a bit used, then I guess you could have mine. In fact, that's why I've come. Chief Hadawa'ko asked me to give it to you. I can't imagine why it was so important to him that you have it. He'd have brought it himself, of course, but he nearly worried himself sick over frightening you. Still, he very much wanted you to have it. It's a silly book, really. No one has ever read it in all these long years. You would be the very first, though I've nearly filled it all up with stories."

"What kind of stories?" Jenny asked.

"Stories about all kinds of wonderful things!" Emma exclaimed. "They're the stories that Chief Hadawa'ko told to me on those nights around the fire. The Chief was our friend. He told me all about how the world began, and how everything came to be. Of course, they're just stories... Indian people have strange and wild ways. Papa allowed him to tell me in spite of that and even said I should write them all down. He said that we all have our God and it doesn't matter so much what you call him, or how you tell the stories, just as long as you do call him. He made me this book to write the stories in. He said it wouldn't be long before they were lost. There was a lot of talk about sending the Indians away."

Emma pressed the wooden box into Jenny's arms.

"Take it. It's yours now."

"Thank you, Emma. Can't you read it to me? I'm not good at reading yet."

"How about I start you off?" Emma suggested. "C'mon, we'll go back to the spring. It'll be cooler there by the water."

Once again holding the candle in front of her, Emma ducked back through the doorway, followed by Jenny. She had gone only a few steps when she stopped suddenly.

"Oh dear," she said and looked more than a little nervous. "I must go now. He's coming!"

"He?" Jenny asked.

"You must go too! Hurry!" She sounded frightened.

"Wait—" Jenny pleaded, but Emma was gone.

Jenny awoke with a start and found herself still sitting in the niche. Looking around quickly, she canvassed the area for 'him', whomever he might be. Seeing no one, she told herself it was just a silly dream. Still, she thought...

Rising up from her seat, she wandered around the corner and into the darkened room where she had stood with Emma moments before. She had no candle this time and could barely see. Feeling around, she located the shelves against the wall and followed them towards the back corner of the room. A thick blanket of dust covered the shelving and she nearly turned back more than once as her hands brushed through sticky cobwebs. But then she touched something else—something hard and rough there on the bottom shelf. The rock!

Jenny made the corner and began to climb the shelves.   One, two, three...and reaching up, her hand found the cold, stone wall. Just a bit to the right maybe, or a bit lower.

Finally, she found what she was searching for. There, just above the fourth shelf she found the void in the wall. She knew the box would be there!

Quickly she reached into the hole and at once felt the smooth wood of the box. But then something scuttled hurriedly across her hand.

"Gah!" she screamed, jerking her hand back. An enormous spider was crawling up her arm and she flung it furiously toward the floor. For a moment, she was thrown horribly off-balance and nearly fell off the shelf. Grabbing it with both hands again, she steadied herself.

It took every bit of nerve that Jenny possessed to reach into the hole again, but reach, she did. As she groped, she found an indentation in the side of the box, just small enough to make a perfect hand-hold and she slid the box out of its hiding place. She moved it down to the second shelf and climbed back down to the floor. She had Emma's box!

Elation set in as she rounded the corner and headed back toward the niche. She couldn't wait to see what was inside.

But the light was better near the water. Forgetting all about the rules, Jenny walked to the ledge of the spring. She had forgotten too, that 'he' was coming and she should make haste. Instead, she sat down on the ledge, as if this were a thing she'd done a million times, and let her feet dangle into the dark water. Beyond cold, the water was freezing, but it was also refreshing and helped wash away the feeling of being covered in cobwebs.

Quickly, Jenny opened the cover of her new book. Although she could barely see in the dim light, she could make out several strange characters written on the first yellowed page:

To my darling, Emma Mae,

From your beloved Papa.

Given with great affection,

This day of our Lord,

September 19, eighteen hundred and twenty four.

Write in happiness!

Darn! She thought. It was written in cursive. Jenny would be unable to read it by herself. She thumbed through the many pages hoping to find something written in the print she was familiar with. As she did this, the temperature by the spring fell rapidly. The temperature fell and the light grew noticeably dimmer. Mesmerized by the flowing characters in the book, Jenny failed to notice the strong smell of sulfur in the air. Shivering once again, she squinted trying to make out the characters. Too late she noticed the changes. Too late she remembered Emma's warning!

She had just decided to get up and leave and was pulling her legs up and out of the water when suddenly she felt a prickling sensation on the back of her neck. Something or someone was behind her! She sensed the blackness of that something deep in the pit of her stomach, and the smell made her belly heave.

Jenny froze. From nowhere, what felt like a pair of strong hands clapped her on the back and pushed hard! The book flew through the air and dropped to the dirt floor as Jenny plunged into the frigid spring. She had just time enough for one loud gasp before she began to sink into the icy, dark water.

Wait! her mind cried out to no one. *I don't know how to swim!*

As Jenny's head went under, she opened her eyes wide. She could see dim light from above and nothing but blackness below. The water was so cold! She struggled against it, kicking wildly and flailing her arms. One hand found purchase on a slimy rock embedded in the wall and she pulled herself up with all of her might.

"Help!" she screamed, as her head broke water and she gulped for air. "Hel—"

"Olley, Olley, in free!" mocked a high pitched, whine of a voice from above her.

Jenny had no words to attach to the shadowy figure standing on the ledge before her. She tried to scream again, but her vocal chords, frozen with fear, could make no sound.

The thing was oddly childlike, although tall, rangy and pathetically thin.

"Wassa madda, Jeeennnnnyy, that wata cold? Do ya want ta play, little girl?"

He bent down, extending his oddly elongated hand over the ledge as if to help her up. Jenny didn't move. Long, slender fingers with filthy, ragged nails tickled her face under her chin. She snapped her head back violently and nearly lost her grip on the ledge.

"C'mon, Jeeennnny! Le's go! I've got big plans for us. BIG!"

He leaned back and spread his arms wide in emphasis. She could see his face now. Like his hands it was oddly elongated. It looked as if it had been stretched; like how your face looked in those trick mirrors in the carnival fun house. His bulging eyes twinkled merrily. Sparse tufts of long, dark hair sprouted here and there.

"Name's Randall an I been waitin' a loooong time to get choo alone!" He snickered a bit and then began to laugh. "Waited a long time to get choo per-i-od!"

Something wet and oily rolled off his face and landed on hers. Jenny looked around for any means of escape but saw none. The ledge on the other side was too far away for her to reach.

"Wassa madda? Cat got ya tongue?"

As he said this, he smiled, revealing a few crooked, yellow teeth and spaces where others had once been. His breath smelled over-sweet and wrapped around her like a blanket, making her want to vomit.

"Mommy!" she screamed, looking around frantically for any sign of help.

"Okay, then, Girly," he said coolly. "I guess you're too purty to play with me. Guess you're too fiiiiine. Well, we'll see 'bout that. We'll see how fiiiiine you look once you been on this side fer a while! I'll bounce you just like a rubber ball, that's what I'll do." And with that, he laid his long fingers over her forehead and gave her another push. "Bouncy, bouncy, Jenny!"

And then she was falling again. Water filled her nose, choking her and stinging her throat and her sinuses. Her chest ached with the pressure, and the water was so cold that her freezing limbs could barely affect movement at all. She could hear her own heartbeat slowing down, the blood in her veins no longer coursing, but rather plodding lazily, and threatening to stop all together.

Death comes to each of us when it will, and unfortunately, for Jenny, the reaper sat both sides of the fence that day. She could either choose to go up again into the cellar with Randall, or down into the freezing blackness. Down to God knows what!

Almost against her will, she fought the water, spiraling down anyways and desperately reaching out for anything to hold on to. She kicked as hard as she could and her foot smashed into rock sending pain shooting up her thin leg. But it was enough to bring her near the surface again. She could see the dim light from above and now, rather than hoping for help, she prayed she'd be alone at the top.

And then she felt hands reaching in and grabbing hold of her shirt. Hands grabbed her by the hair and dragged her up and out of the freezing pool. She steeled herself against the grimy feel of Randall's long fingers. He had her then!

But these were warm hands--Bethy's hands and Bonny's hands.

"Ouch!" She hollered, and lapsed into a fit of coughing and choking. "Let... go... my hair!"

"Oh, my God, Jenny! What are you doing down here? You could have died!" Beth looked furious bending down before her.

"Nothing." Jenny didn't like being in trouble one bit. Water poured off of the pitiful girl.

"How did you get in here?" Bonny demanded. "How did you get in there?" She pointed at the spring. "If we hadn't come along when we did and heard you screaming—"

"Somebody pushed me," Jenny said. As she spoke, realization dawned and her face contorted with horror. "Randall pushed me in there." Tears rolled down her already wet cheeks and she began to sob.

"Who the heck is Randall? There's no one down here but us, Jenny, and if Mommy finds out you were down here, she'll kill you herself."

Beth obviously didn't believe that Jenny had been pushed.

"She'll kill us all. You know better than to be down here, Jenny."

Jenny could take no more. She threw her arms around Beth's neck, hugging her tightly.

"Geez, that's cold!" Beth shrieked, but she didn't let go.

"Take me out, Bethy, please," Jenny pleaded. "Take me out and I'll never come back down here. I promise. I don't like it down here anymore." It sounded like ennnymooorre through the sobs.

"Let's get her out of here," Bonny said. "Let's get her upstairs and make sure she's all right. We can sneak her in the back."

"If we get caught—"

"We won't," said Bonny.

"Wait!" Jenny cried remembering her book. She freed herself long enough to pack the book back into its box and held on tightly. "Will you carry me? I'm colddd." Her lips were blue and her teeth were chattering.

From a darkened corner on the far side of the basement, Jenny saw Randall watching her. She didn't wait to be carried. Jenny ran.

***

"I believe that was the first day I turned the cows out into that pasture to drink," Eddie said.

CHAPTER SEVEN

This is like gawking at a train wreck, Father Murphy thought. The longer Eddie went on, the more horrified he became. Yet he couldn't have left now if he'd tried. And mercilessly, Eddie went on.

"Before I did that, I cleared it with Charles. I told him about the pool and we walked out there together. When he saw the thing, he looked like a man who'd finally caught a break. He bent down and cupped his hands, doing what I hadn't thought to do. He filled them up and drank from them. When he had done, he looked satisfied.

"'That's damned good, for water, Eddie,' he said.

"And it must have been, because after that he took to filling his thermos from that little pool just about every day. He said that water just tasted sweeter. The cows seemed to like it all right.

"I also used that water to fill up the bull's trough. The bull? He had his own pasture very near to the little pool. We had to keep him separate from the herd, primarily because he didn't need to come in with the rest to be milked, but also because he was one mean son-of-a-bitch. And big too. Even as bulls go, this bastard was a big one.

"Adam started work right on schedule. I had thought that Charles would spend the summer keeping Adam and Ruthy as far apart as possible, but that isn't the way it happened.

In fact, it was almost as if he encouraged them to spend every minute they could together. He often sent Adam to help Ruthy do her chores. Anyone who didn't know him better would have thought he was doing a really nice thing. If I thought it was strange at the time, then I didn't think on it long. There was just way too much to do around the place before haying season began. Looking back though, I have to wonder if he was just giving them enough rope, so to speak. He had to have suspected something.

"Still, if you'd have seen the way Ruthy started to open up...it was like she blossomed overnight. I figured out what was going on right away, but I sure as hell wasn't going to say nothin'. Adam was a nice kid. He brought a lot of life to the family. Everybody loved him. And, it made my heart happy to see the way Ruthy smiled when she was with him."

***

Later that evening, after dinner, the four youngest girls were gathered in the room that Beth and Bonny shared. Jenny had long since been warm and dry again and the incident in the cellar all but forgotten. Dawny was lying across Beth's bed near to the foot, Emma's wooden box lying in front of her. Beth and Jenny lay side by side, propped up on the pillows, against the headboard. Bonny sat cross-legged, Indian style on the tattered throw rug to one side. Beth was reading aloud from Emma's journal:

How Chipmunk Got His Stripes

As told to Emma Mae Ten Broek

By Hadawa'ko, Chief of the Tuscarora

Long ago, before the animals lost their

ability to speak,--

"Wait! Animals could talk?" Dawny asked, puzzled.

"Maybe," Jenny said, "A long time ago, when Indians lived here."

"Indians lived *here*?" Dawny asked again.

"Shush up, Dawny!" Jenny answered. "Just listen to the story."

Beth resumed reading:

Long ago, before the animals lost their

ability to speak, there lived a very large

bear. The bear was strong and proud.

"I am the most important of animals,"

said the bear. "I can do anything I wish,

though the other animals cannot."

"Did you ever see a real bear?" asked Dawny.

"Dawny! Shush, for heaven's sake!" cried Jenny. Beth sighed and began again:

A mischievous chipmunk overheard the bear talking to himself.

"Is that so?" he asked.

"Yes," said the bear, spying the chipmunk. And he rolled over a large log with a single paw just to prove it. "You should fear me just as the others do," he said.

"I'm afraid of bears," said Dawny. "They're mean."

"Do you want to hear the story, or not?" Beth asked.

"Are there any pictures?"

"Dawny, come on!"

"Okay, okay," Dawny answered. "You don't got to get all grumpy about it!"

Beth went on:

"Are you sure that you can do ANYTHING?" asked the chipmunk. "Can you stop the sun from rising in the sky in the morning?"

Dawny giggled. "No one could do that."

"DAWNY!" the three girls cried in unison.

"Okay, okay. Sshssshhhh," Dawny said, putting her forefinger to her lips. Beth went on:

The bear thought about this for a moment, but he was sure of himself. If he could not do it, then it could not be done.

"I have never tried to stop the sun," he answered, "but I believe that I could if I wanted to."

"Are you sure?" asked the chipmunk. "I should dearly like to see that."

The bear answered confidently, "I, Bear, say that I am sure. Tomorrow, come early to the clearing in the wood, and you shall see that the sun will not rise in the sky."

The bear sat thinking late into the night. The little chipmunk curled up in its nest, laughing at the silly bear, and finally slept. The bear thought and thought, and at last decided to speak to the sun.

"You will not rise today," he said. "You will not rise." He repeated this phrase over and over, sure that it would work—

"Oh, that's not gonna do it," said Dawny.

"That's it!" said Beth. "I'm done." She folded the book closed and began to get up.

"Wait!" cried Jenny. "Don't stop reading. Come on, Bethy, we can't read it by ourselves, it's in cursive. Please?"

"I'll be quiet now," Dawny promised. "I won't talk no more."

"If you do," Jenny began, "I'll—"

"Well I said I won't." she answered curtly.

"Okay, then," Beth answered and sat back again. "I'd like to get to the end of this." She tried again:

However, the sun came up anyway, just as it always had.

"I knew it!"

"DAWNY!"

Dawn began to pout but she remained silent for the remainder of the story.

Chipmunk was delighted and began running around in circles, teasing the bear.

"Sun is stronger than bear," he laughed. "Bear tried all night, but the sun came up in spite of him! Bear is not the strongest. Sun is stronger than bear."

The proud bear became angry now. Quick as a wink, he lashed out and captured the foolish chipmunk in his large paw. He pinned the chipmunk to the ground.

Dawny looked as though she were going to burst, but she said nothing.

"The sun may be stronger than me," he said, "but you are not. And when Sun comes up tomorrow, you will not be here to see him!"

The chipmunk, having seen the error of his ways, tried to reason with Bear. "You are right, Bear, you are the strongest and the fastest of all the animals. Forgive me, I was only teasing you."

But the angry bear was not amused. He did not release the chipmunk.

"Please, Bear, I am sorry," said the chipmunk, but to no avail.

Jenny glanced over the top of the book to see Dawny gnawing on her fingernails. Still, she remained quiet.

"Well, then, at least let me say a prayer to the creator before you kill me," pleaded chipmunk.

"I shall let you pray," Bear said, "But do it quickly. Your time to walk the sky road has come!"

"I should like to do that," said the chipmunk, "but you are holding me so tightly that I cannot breathe. How can I say a prayer if I can hardly squeak? If you could loosen your paw just a little, then surely I could catch a breath. Then I will say my last prayer to the Maker of All."

Bear lifted his paw but just a tiny bit. That little bit was enough though, and the chipmunk squeezed out of his predicament and ran for his safe hole in the ground. When Bear saw what was happening, he swung his giant paw at the chipmunk and the tips of his sharp claws scratched the length of chipmunk's back, leaving three long scratch marks. And to this day, Chipmunks around the world wear those scars to remind them what happens when one animal makes fun of another.

"Well, that was a good story," announced Dawn.

"Yeah," Jenny agreed, "when you finally stopped talking."

"Shut up, Jenny. You're mean."

"And you are a pain in the kadiddlehopper, Dawny!" The older girls laughed at the term borrowed from a popular TV show. Annette said it all the time but it sounded so funny coming from their little sister.

"You shut up, Jenny! You shouldn't make fun. You'd have known that if you'd listened to the story!"

"Me? You're the one who was chattering the whole time."

"Uh, uh, Jenny. You're just jealous of me!"

"Quit arguing, you two," cautioned Beth.

"Besides," said Jenny, "you're not making any sense at all, Dawny."

"Uh huh, yes I am. Hey! What else is in this box?" Dawny sat up and opened the box.

Jenny, in a mood now, was no longer willing to share.

"Put it down, Dawny, it's mine."

Dawny ignored this and began poking through the box's contents.

"What's this?" she pulled out the feather quill.

"Put it back!" Jenny cried, getting to her feet now. She began to advance on her sister.

"Quit it!" yelled Beth.

"I ain't gonna put it back," said Dawny, standing up on the bed now as well. "It's mine now, you stupid dummy-head!"

"You're gonna get it," Jenny promised.

"No, I ain't," countered Dawny. "You're not the boss of me!"

"You wanna bet?" Jenny gave Dawny a good, solid push, sending her tumbling off the bed. The box careened to the floor ahead of her and landed in several pieces. Jenny jumped off the bed on top of Dawny, ready to fight further if need be.

"Jenny!" screamed Beth and Bonny simultaneously. Bonny pulled Jenny off of Dawn who was now crying hysterically.

"Owwwwwww! You broke me! My leg hurrrrrts!"

"I'm gonna break you, you little brat!"

"JENNY! You settle down right now," demanded Bonny. "You're going to get us in trouble."

Just then, the sound of footsteps echoed in the hall outside. Four sets of eyes looked nervously towards the door. At once it opened and Callie walked into the room.

"You guys had better shut up before Mommy and Daddy hear you. What's going on in here anyways? What's wrong with Dawny?"

Jenny put her head down and studied the floor.

"Jenny?" Callie asked.

"She fell off the bed."

"LIAR!" Dawny shouted. "She pushed me."

"Did not! You fell, cuz you're a baby!" And the two were at it again. The three older girls quickly rounded up the two younger ones, who looked extremely unhappy at being restrained. Jenny, looking once more at the floor, now noticed the pieces of the box lying there.

"You broke my box," she cried.

Dawn looked down in horror.

"I'm sorrrry, Jenny. I didn't mean to," she whined. "I didn't mean to break it."

Callie bent to pick up the pieces.

"Where did you get this?" she wondered and began picking through its contents. The other girls went quiet. "Where'd this stuff come from?"

"Jenny found it," Beth admitted. "There's a book too." She handed over the journal.

"What do you mean, found it?" Callie asked. "Found it, where?"

Beth and Bonnie looked at one another and then at Jenny and Dawny.

"It was in the back of Jenny's closet," Bonny lied. She was taking no chances that Annette would find out they'd been in the cellar. "Who knows where it came from? It could have been in there forever."

"Weird," Callie said, as she opened the book. "Whoa! This book is old. Look at the date!"

"Yeah, we know," said Beth. "We've been reading the stories to the girls. That is until they tried to kill each other."

140

"Wow," said Callie, "and all this junk was in the box with the book?"

"It's not junk," Jenny protested. "It's mine!"

"I broke Jenny's box," Dawny wailed.

"Shhhh," Callie said, setting the book to one side. "I don't think it's broken. It just came apart is all. Don't worry, Dawny, we'll fix it."

Callie began picking up the pieces. The box was in fact, not broken. The top portion—the tray that had housed the book and the pen—had merely fallen out. Underneath was another compartment.

"See? It all goes right back together," Callie said. She placed the top tray back in the box and began picking up the strewn items. "This stuff is cool, Jenny."

Beth and Bonny released the two younger girls, who began to help Callie.

"Wow, look at this!" Callie said, holding up a silver chain. Attached to the chain was an arrowhead, but this one was not crafted from slate or black stone as those her father collected from the fields were. This one was made from some white material, resembling finely polished bone. She whistled as she turned the object over in her hands.

"Hey! Lemme see that!" Jenny exclaimed. "That wasn't in here before!"

"It must have come out of the secret compartment," reasoned Beth.

On the front of the white arrowhead, the image of a great tree had been lovingly hand-carved.

"Wow, this is really nice," said Callie. "I like it a lot."

"Can I have it, Jenny?" Dawny asked. "Please? Please, please, pleeeaase?"

"Why should I give it to you? You almost broke my box."

"Please, Jenny, I really like it a lot," Dawny pleaded. Her expression was both earnest and sincere. "What are you going to do with it, if I can't have it?"

"I know what I'll do. I'm going to give it to Ruthy, since she didn't like her other birthday present. Do you think she'll like this, Callie?"

"Yeah, I do. Who wouldn't like this? It's beautiful. I wonder who made it? It looks old."

"Chief Hadawa'ko made it for Emma, I bet," Jenny said.

"Chief Who? Who's Emma?"

Having talked her way right into a corner now, Jenny related her 'dream' to her sisters. The four of them listened raptly, and even Dawny was quiet now. She told them almost everything, although she avoided any mention of the cellar. Callie may well have assumed that the box was found in the back of the closet. Jenny also avoided speaking of Randall. Beth hadn't believed that part of the story earlier and there was no reason to think that the others would believe it now. Jenny shivered just thinking about the creepy man-thing in the cellar.

"Wow," said Callie, when Jenny had finished the telling, "that's really weird. Mommy always says that real Indians lived here once. What's that story she's always telling, Bethy? The one about the Chief who got killed down by the lake?"

"Oh, I know what one you mean," Beth answered. "The one about the treasure buried here on the farm someplace? Didn't she say it's buried under three stalks of Asparagus planted in a triangle? And supposedly the ghost of that old Chief comes back once a year and makes sure his treasure hasn't been dug up."

"Yeah, that's the story," Callie said. "Daddy's been looking for years, but he's never found anything yet. Course, by now, the Asparagus is long gone."

"So do you think Ruthy would like this then?" Jenny asked.

"Yeah."

"Why does Ruthy gotta get all the presents? Just cuz she had a stupid birthday, and now she's sooooo special," Dawny whined. "I want a necklace too."

"Awww, Dawny, you want everything," Jenny groaned. "Don't you want Ruthy to be happy?"

"Yeah," she sighed. And then, "But I brought her all those poppies. That shoulda been enough, by the Jesus!"

The other four girls burst out laughing and it was decided. The necklace was to be given to Ruthy that very night.

A few minutes later the girls listened as Callie's footfalls made their way down the hall towards her bedroom. Only this time, they clearly heard two sets instead of just one.

***

In the meantime, Ruthy had been outside in the yard with Adam. It was one of those lovely, clear evenings, when the moon is full and there are a million stars in the sky. These are the evenings when it seems that a universal switch has been thrown and the hustle and bustle of a hectic day is silenced, making way for the magic hush of nighttime. These are the evenings when we cannot help holding hands and whispering secrets.

Adam and Ruthy spent the warm, summer night catching fireflies in a jar. Just that and no more. They didn't speak of troubles, or of heartaches. Rather they laughed and played like the children that they were--like the children that they should have been.

When Ruthy went to bed that night, she was happier than she'd ever been before. As she lay in her darkened room, she watched the dreamy moon outside her window and thought about the future. She dreamed of becoming Mrs. Adam Morris. She could wear the new birthday dress for the ceremony. She knew exactly how she'd fix her hair and she might even wear makeup! It all seemed so close now...so real.

The bottle of fireflies sat on her windowsill, tiny, red and green sparks flitting about like fireworks against the deep blue sky. She rubbed the arrowhead necklace between her fingers and drifted off peacefully, knowing for the first time, that she really was loved.

CHAPTER EIGHT

"The next couple of weeks on the farm flew by. It was if a great change had come over the place. The children had taken on the happy air of those freed from school for the summer. Ruthy wore a perpetual smile as she and Adam worked dutifully, side by side throughout the long, hot days. Even Annette seemed a bit more relaxed. It was little things mostly, like letting the laundry go for a few minutes in order to stop and read a book to the little ones or coming outside to join them in a game of marbles or hopscotch, which was their favorite."

Eddy smiled at the memory.

"But the biggest change was the one that came over Charles. It was like he was giddy! He worked tirelessly, without complaining or snapping at the farm-hands. He said 'please' and 'thank you' when he wanted something from the dinner table instead of just pointing and grunting as was his usual way. He became infernally optimistic about things— always taking the high road when discussing the business of the farm, no matter how dim things might look. He even played with the kids quite a bit.

"And I know it had something to do with that water. The more he drank of it, the more he wanted. Some days, I swear that I saw him fill that thermos of his five or six times. It must have agreed with the cattle too since milk production went way up. I never enjoyed working on the farm so much as in those last few weeks.

"The water...not one time did I ever see Charles sharing with any of the others. In that, at least, he hadn't changed. It was like he was afraid that it would run dry. But thank God above for small favors."

Father Murphy shook his head in agreement.

"The kids made a nightly ritual out of reading from Emma's journal. It was in this way that Jenny and Dawny learned about the Indian culture. Native American, I guess you'd call it now, but back then we always called them Indians.

"They learned the Indian version of the story of creation. And you'll excuse me here, Father, if this doesn't agree with your own version, but this is the way it was written in the book. Some nights I could hear them reading out loud through my bedroom wall.

"They read that in the beginning there was no Earth. There was the Sky World above, where human type beings lived, and the Water World below. They learned how the brother of Sky Woman uprooted the Tree of Life and found a huge hole beneath it. Sky Woman fell through the hole and floated down towards the water. The birds and water dwellers from the water world feared for her life. Many birds gathered to break her fall, but there was no Earth to set her upon. Instead, they laid her gently on the back of a giant sea turtle.

"The water dwellers believed that Sky Woman needed land to live on, so they dove to great depths looking for dirt. All of the animals failed save the little muskrat. He was able to bring forth a tiny pile of earth in his small paws and lay it on the turtle's back. From this dirt grew Turtle Island, known to us as the Earth.

"Soon, Sky woman gave birth to a daughter. The daughter of Sky Woman married the West Wind and gave birth to twins. The first, born the normal way was called the Right-Handed Twin. The second was not born normally, though it didn't say how he was born. It did say though, that his mother died bearing him and afterward he was called the Left-Handed Twin.

"Both twins were endowed with special powers. The Right-handed Twin created everything on Earth that is gentle and beautiful. He created the streams and the flowers, the hills and the butterflies, the plants and the earth formations. The Left-Handed Twin created darker things. He placed the thorns on the rose bushes. He set the snake to crawling. He created thunder and then lightening after that.

"Together, the twins created mankind. They taught him diplomacy and conflict resolution. But they also taught him war. Gentleness and anger, love and hate. Each of these things, both good and bad, was no more than a natural part of this Earth. And since their differences caused it to be impossible for them to live together, they divided the Earth into realms. The Right-Handed Twin lived in the daylight world while the Left-Handed Twin became a creature of the night.

"The girls also learned how the four winds were named. They learned the origin of the Pleiades. They read about Wah-kon-Tah, the Great Spirit, and other spirits too. There were many stories, some of them funny, little animal tales such as: 'How Bear Lost His Tail', and 'Why Owl Has Big Eyes'. Others taught morals and character like the story of 'The Girl Who Was Not Satisfied with Simple Things' and 'Ahneah, the Rose Flower'. Obviously, Chief Hadawa'ko had schooled Emma well in the ways of the Indian people because there were so many lessons. There were even stories about Deganawada, the Peacemaker, who, along with Hiawatha worked to bring the several nations of the Iroquois Confederacy together under the Great Law of Peace.

"Emma had also written a lot about the village of Chief Hadawa'ko. She wrote about how the women of the tribe chose the leaders. She described the longhouses that the Iroquois lived in. She wrote about lacrosse and other games they played. She told about the three sisters; corn, beans, and squash, who nourished the tribe when the hunting was scarce. And she explained how the tribe traded beaver and bearskins for knives, beads and trinkets."

Father Murphy fought down the urge to inquire if the family still had the book. He would love to have a look at an artifact like that.

Eddie didn't notice, and went on speaking instead.

"Jenny and Dawny loved those stories. All the girls did. They took to those Indian stories like they were born into it! And if you saw them playing Cowboys and Indians in the yard, it was always Mark who was the cowboy. The girls no longer wanted any part of that role.

"'I am Haudenosaunee,' Jenny would holler. Haudenosaunee is the name the Iroquois call themselves by. 'I was not born in America! America was born on my land!'

"All in all, things were going great. But there was one thing that wouldn't get right. Remember I told you about the photographic image that I began to see in my head when I looked straight on at the house? You know— the one that had begun to get black and white on the left edge? I tried my darnedest to make this not so, but it was what it was and it was not going away. Every evening when I came out of the barn and headed towards the house, there it was...that barely perceptible shift, like a faint clicking sound inside my head, and then the smallest amount of color would drain right out of that picture and every time a little bit more of it would turn to black and white. And what's worse, I started seeing things that weren't even there in real life. Shrubs and such mostly, at first. But then I started seeing people who didn't belong there. I knew they weren't real because of the way they were dressed--old-fashioned and all--and because they were black and white too. They never moved or spoke. Just kind of stood there, staring at me and frozen in time.

"I reasoned that the problem was with my eyes, but then it didn't happen with anything else or at any other time. I blamed it on the sun like the way you sometimes see white spots swimming through the air after looking directly into a bright light. I came up with a few different excuses, but nothing rang true.

"It was right about then that I started going into town after work, to the Library. Old Mr. Walters, the town Historian who ran the place, had always been fond of me. He let me in after closing and showed me how to look things up. I needed to know the history of the place. The truth about things, you know? And it didn't take us long to find the documents."

Father Murphy leaned forward in his chair. True or not, this was a good story.

"Over the years," Eddie continued, "a lot of people lived and died there. The house and barn were both built way back when the town was first settled in the 1800's. It was mostly just Indians prior to that, and many remained there alongside the first settlers for some time. Every year, come time to plow, we'd find dozens of arrowheads and such in the newly dug furrows.

"We found an old newspaper article that told about how the farm was once used as a poorhouse for the indigent. Now, 'indigent', back in the early 1900's, most surely meant something quite different than you might suppose. 'Indigent' covered a whole range of sins. Some of those people were just plain penniless and needed feeding. Some were lazy n'er-do-wells and wouldn't work a job. But a lot of them were just not right in the head. We'd call them mentally challenged today, but back then they might have been called 'retards' or even 'idiots'. I don't guess it matters what they were called, the point is they weren't able to make a living for themselves.

"Others were just plain crazy, near as I can figure," he went on. "Back then there weren't any fancy institutions, so these people were sent to local poorhouses to be taken care of.

"Something must have gone wrong though because The Great State of New York, in 1919, interceded on behalf of the indigents, and they opened up an investigation. What they found there was treated as criminal. Inhuman is more like it. The state found horrible living conditions; holes in the walls big enough that snow was actually drifting into filthy, freezing sleeping quarters, food gone rancid and full of worms, and screaming , half-starved patients chained to steel rings up in the attic."

"Good Lord!" Father Murphy interjected. "Those poor souls."

"Yep. They shut the place right down and brought those people out of there. The ones that made it, at least. The state filed charges and the guy that owned the place went to jail. Probably went straight to hell after, though that's pure-damned speculation on my part. I do that a lot. Some of what I'm telling you is stuff I figured out a lot later, just from talking to the kids and comparing notes. And maybe you won't believe any of it. Some of it even seems crazy to me. But I've had a lot of years to think on this, and I'm pretty sure that all of it is the truth, or as near as I can get to it.

"In the end, I really thought that I must have a screw loose or something and that worried me to no end. That wasn't something you'd want people to know about back then so I didn't say anything about it to anyone. I didn't tell a soul. But every time I saw it happen a chill went right through me, I swear! And sometimes I lay awake at night wondering just what would happen when that picture finally went all the way over to black and white? What in the name of all that's holy, could it mean?"

CHAPTER NINE

"And just as quickly as things had turned around and looked better for a time, they changed direction again and headed south in a hurry. Charles became a ceaseless whir of energy. Except all of the feeling good and being nice went south along with the rest of it. To the extent that he was driven, he drove everyone else in front of him. And he drove them like cattle. If he'd been brutal in the past, that brutality now increased ten-fold. He became determined to go over every inch of

161

the place, cleaning, painting, and fixing-up until it was once more in mint condition. This was no small feat considering the size of the place and the amount of work to be done just in keeping with the daily chores, without adding on all of the extra things.

"Ruthy and Adam were given the chore of scrubbing down the entire milk-house. And when I say 'scrubbing down' I mean washing with bleach, scrubbing until their hands bled and there was a spit shine on everything. Afterwards, they were to whitewash it. That probably would've been enough to keep them busy for weeks, but it wasn't enough for Charles. He also wanted the rest of the barn scraped and re-painted.

"Me and the other hired men rode all 360 acres of fence-line, setting every inch to right. We also shoveled and scraped the entire barn, washing out mangers, restacking hay up in the mow, oiling and doing maintenance on all of the farm equipment, painting and anything else he came up with.

"Mark was sent to clean out and organize the garage. As I may have mentioned before, the garage was as big as any house and filled with every kind of tool and piece of hardware you could imagine. Mark wouldn't be playing Cowboys and Indians for a while.

"Callie, Beth and Bonny each had to pick up a lot more of the regular chores--the care and feeding of all of the animals and such--so that the rest of us could get more done on our own projects. Everyone worked together to get the milking done twice a day."

Father Murphy tried to imagine how it was back then. Those poor children!

"Annette's chores didn't change radically. There was only so much time in a day and between her job, and all that she was already doing, there wasn't much more you could squeeze out of her. Instead, what she got as Charles' mood turned sour was a constant litany of pissing and moaning. He bitched at that poor woman from sun-up to sun-up again. There wasn't anything she could do that was right by him. I honestly don't know why she didn't kill him right then, but she didn't.

"And I could've said something, but I didn't. I'd just be standing there, feeling like a first class idiot, watching him go up one side of her and down the other. I'd see her lips pressed tightly together as she labored to hold her tongue. I could see the muscles in the side of her face working furiously whenever he was at her. She literally walked on egg shells around him and shuffled the kids from here to there, trying to keep them busy and out of his way. The excuses she made for him rained down like dead leaves in Autumn.

"'Charles isn't feeling well today.' She'd say.

"Or, 'Charles is under a lot of stress,'

"Or, 'Be quiet, kids, your father is trying to think about important things right now.'

"Jenny and Dawn were sent to clean up the front yard and pick up any toys or odd junk that had been strewn about. Every single one of us was working his hardest. And Charles never even began to get satisfied with the jobs we did. But the worst of it was the way he talked to those children! He treated the animals better!

"He'd say, 'You goddamned, worthless Sons-a-Bitches! Things are going to change around here, by the Jesus! Now move! Double-time!'

"It was then that I started thinking about where he'd come from, ya know? Charles Barnes came from good German stock. That was on his mother's side of the family. Her maiden name was Schmitz. The way he ordered everyone around and abused everyone and everything, I thought there was a good chance that it was the same German blood as those that had recently gassed six or seven million Jews in Europe."

165

Father Murphy could only shake his head. This story got so much worse as it went along.

"Double-time it was too, as they ran to do whatever it was that he demanded.

"Of course, hindsight is twenty-twenty and looking back, I can see where I went wrong. I can see how this is the place where I should have stepped in and done something. The thing is though, say any word, give him the least bit of a hard time and he just got worse. The monster in him grew by leaps and bounds, and you just knew if you said anything that things would only get harder on everyone. So we tread carefully around him, worked until we could work no more and prayed he'd wake up in a better mood the following morning.

"The cows too, started growing restless. At first, it was little things like instead of waiting for us to ring that bell summoning them to the barn to be milked, they'd show up there early, all by themselves, bags swollen with milk, and bawling to the high heavens to be relieved of it.

And because their bags were tender, they began to kick at us when we were putting on the milking machines. They'd snort and blow and act for all the world like they were just plain pissed off at everything. Now that's not right. As I said before, cows are stupid creatures. Normally, they just don't give a shit about anything.

"And then I knew for sure that there was something wrong with the water in that little pool. I did speak up about that.

"'Charles,' I said, 'I think that there's something wrong with that water. Have you noticed how the cows have been acting lately?' I knew better than to mention the change in *his* behavior.

"'Them cows are doing just fine, Ed,' he answered. 'Making more milk than two herds ought to. Seeing that bulk tank truck come twice a week to pick up the milk instead of once makes me nothing but happy.'

"I tried again. 'I could take some uptown and see if I could get it tested, just to be sure—'

"'Ed. Do you get your paycheck every goddamned Friday? Have I ever missed giving you your paycheck?'

"He was getting madder by the minute.

"'No, Sir,' I answered.

"'Then how about you just mind your own goddamned business and go on about doing what gets you that paycheck to begin with, huh?'

"That was the last I said about that. But again, looking back, I think he knew. He had to have known something wasn't right.

"It was true, though, even if it wasn't right. That fancy, silver, bulk-tank truck was coming a lot more often and I supposed this month's milk check was going to be a whopper. Maybe that would settle him down a bit, I thought. Maybe that would make him happy."

***

The heat of the July sun was merciless and it beat down upon Ruthy and Adam like a pestilence. Hot and humid, and filled with the strong smell of bleach, the air was heavy and difficult to breathe. They scrubbed the exterior of the milk-house to the accompaniment of the songs blaring from Adam's transistor radio. As they worked, they played a game based on the music they were listening to. The object was to name both the singer and the song title, and to be the first one to do that. Two points were given for right answers. Adam, who was nothing if not a music enthusiast, had a healthy lead. It seemed as though he knew everything about every song ever written.

The radio began, "*She loves you, yeah—*"

"The Beatles!" Ruthy cried. "She Loves You, Yeah, Yeah, Yeah!"

"Ten point gimmee," Adam responded. "What took you so long?"

"What's taking you so long?" Ruthy teased. "You've been cleaning that same section for an hour."

"Just trying to stay as close to you as possible, Girl," he answered.

His long, dark hair had been tied back under a bandanna and that, combined with acutely blue eyes and strong, angular features caused him to look as if he'd just stepped out of a gypsy caravan. No farmer, he.

"Better get a move on," Ruthy said, "or we'll never get finished."

"She loves me, yeah, yeah, yeah," Adam sang, still working on the same section of wall. "I'm winning, yeah, yeah, yeah."

Ruthy rolled her eyes, groaned, and continued scrubbing as the song played out.

After a few words from a faceless DJ, a female voice came over the radio, "*Is she really going out with him?*" the voice asked.

Another girl answered, "*Well there she is, let's ask her!*"

"Oh! I know this one!" Ruthy shouted. "It's...it's..."

"Come on," Adam said, "you can get this one."

"*Betty, is that Jimmy's ring you're wearing?*" the radio voice asked.

"*Mmm hmmm,*" the girl answered.

"It's..." Ruthy sighed, "Oh man! I know I know this one!"

Adam grinned and waited patiently for her answer.

"*I met him in the candy store,*" the voice crooned. "*He turned around and smiled at me. You get the picture?*"

"*Yes we see.*"

"*That's why I fell for—*"

"THE LEADER OF THE PACK!" Ruthy shouted. "Woo-hoo! I got it!"

"Uh, not so fast there, little Lady," Adam said doing his best John Wayne impression. "The group was?"

"Oh no," Ruthy groaned. "It's...it's...geez, Adam, I got the song. Can I just get one point?"

"The Shangri-las wouldn't like that one bit, now would they?" he teased.

"My folks were always putting him down," Ruthy sang. She turned and pointed at Adam as she sang, "They said he came from the wrong side of town."

She didn't know the next few lines but filled them in with duh, duh, duh, hmmm, hmmm. The sound of a revving motorcycle engine screamed in the background of the song.

"Pathetic, Ruthy," Adam laughed, as she went on.

"I'll never forget you, the leader of the pack!" Ruthy definitely finished on a high note--high and about ten notches west of in tune.

"Ouch!" Adam cried, covering both ears with his dripping wet hands. "My ears are bleeding!"

"Good," Ruthy said. "Maybe you won't be able to get the next one either."

***

Jenny and Dawny, on this particular day, had been sent to pull weeds in Annette's prize, half-acre garden on the east side of the house. Charles had ushered them out early this morning and given them their first lesson in weeding. At the beginning of each row there was a stake with a seed packet stapled to it identifying the plants in that row. They had only to pull those weeds growing in between the rows. The plants were well into their season and had grown thick and lush. Here were the peas, beans and cauliflower that would nourish the family in hearty stews throughout the long winter ahead. Green tomatoes hung on heavily laden vines which had been carefully staked for support. Tiny cucumbers sprouted from amongst the rows and the purple and orange tops of carrots and beets peeked out from their underground hiding places. Hills of squash, potatoes and melons ran through the back corner of the garden like the gentle waves of a low tide ocean. The corn had already grown tall—about two and a half feet—providing a natural wall on one side, giving shade and a sense of seclusion from the rest of the farm. Just beyond the garden lay a natural outcropping of forest adding to that sense.

They'd been out there for two sweaty hours already, and had barely made a dent. Dawny, having grown bored long ago, had made half a dozen trips to the house for 'a dwink', or to 'go potty', each time taking just a bit longer to return. She had been lying on her stomach following the progress of a wayward ant when she noticed the bright, pinkish-red tip of a radish sticking out of the ground. Annette's tattered and much too large gardening gloves adorned her small hands. Curiosity had her in its grip and she brushed at the soil near the top of the root, exposing more and more of it as she rubbed. Finally, she could stand it no more and she plucked it free.

"What do ya spose this is, Jenny?" she asked, sitting up.

Never having been involved with the actual preparation of vegetables, neither of the girls was very familiar with how they looked in their raw form.

Jenny was on her bare knees in the dirt tugging steadily at the weeds in the next row. "Hey!" she shouted. "You're not supposed to be picking the vegetables. You're supposed to be picking the weeds. You're gonna get in a lot of trouble, Dawny."

"Well, they won't know if you don't tell them, so hush it up! And anyways, I just wanted to know what it is."

"I don't know, but I bet it's nasty."

"Ya think so?"

"It's here in the garden, ain't it? All this stuff is yucky."

"Nuh uh, Jenny. Them strawberries is really yummy." She flicked a bit of loose soil off the radish with one floppy, gloved finger.

Jenny considered this for a moment before answering, "Yeah, that's true. I don't know, maybe it'll be all right."

"It looks pretty," Dawny said and began to polish the thing with the bottom of her shirt.

"Well, go ahead then, eat it."

"You try it first," Dawny suggested. She looked hopeful as she held it out for her sister to take. "It's all clean now."

"Uh uh, Dawny. You picked it. Now you gotta eat it."

"Please? I'm getting hungry, but I don't wanna eat it if it's yucky."

"No way," Jenny answered.

"Okay, then," Dawny scolded, "but you're gonna be sorry, cuz it's gonna be good and great! And I ain't gonna share with you then cuz it's gonna be all gone and you can just get your own, Jenny!"

She jammed the radish into her mouth and began chewing enthusiastically. At first. All too soon though, her face contorted as the heat of the radish bit at her tender tongue.

"Ugh," she sputtered and began to spit the hot, purple and white bits back out onto the ground. She scraped wildly at her tongue with the dirty gloves. "That's yucky! Someone oughta teach Mommy how to grow a good garden cuz I don't think she knows very much about this stuff!"

Jenny giggled. "Told you so, Dawny."

"Yuck, it burns," she cried, "Now I gotta go back in the house and get another drink of water." And off she ran.

Jenny sighed and lay back in the cool soil. She liked the garden, liked the feel of the loose dirt between her fingers and toes. And while she'd have had a hard time expressing it in words, she liked the feeling of the partnership between herself and nature. There was a trustworthy feeling of give and take, of asking and receiving, and as long as she did her part for that garden then it would give right back to her. It was a place where things happened just as they were supposed to and she took comfort in that.

Moments later, Dawny skipped barefooted back into the garden patch. The front of her shirt was wet from a drink gone askew and her shorts hung crooked on her small frame.

"Are we all done yet?" she asked.

Jenny rose to her feet and stretched. "Nah, Dawny. It'll take at least all day, maybe more."

"Awww, don't say that, Jenny. I'm all tired out of this weeding business. Let's do somethin' funner."

"Papa would like this very much," came a voice from an adjoining cornrow. "It's an excellent plot, wouldn't you say, Chief?"

Jenny and Dawny looked on as Emma and a strange, dark-skinned man stepped into the row they now occupied. Emma looked exactly as Jenny remembered her from the basement that day; beautifully groomed blonde hair tied up in a bow and a frock made of white, eyelet lace. Her skin, however, looked much paler in the sunlight. She was followed by a slender, well muscled, young man, with thoughtful, dark eyes, and chiseled features. His head had been shaved for the most part, save for two thin braids which sprouted from the top of it and grew down past his right shoulder. White, black and purple beads weighted down the strands. A trio of colored feathers jutted straight up from the crown of his head like plumage. He wore a buck-skin loin-cloth that had been dyed to a mossy green, the tops of his thighs peeking out of tan leather leggings. A bright red length of rough fabric about two yards long encircled his waist and hung down again on his right side like a cummerbund. The ends of this were also embellished with colored beads. Beneath his knees were tied two inch wide strips of a similar red fabric. Silver bands adorned his forearms and wrists, and around his neck hung an oval pendant carved from bone just as Ruthy's was, and bearing the image of the same tree. His feet were bare.

"Emma!" Jenny cried.

"Yikes! Indians!" Dawny exclaimed. For a moment, she looked as if she was going to run, but a reassuring glance from Jenny stopped her feet.

"Miss Jenny Barnes, I'd like to introduce you to my friend, Chief Hadawa'ko" said Emma proudly. "Chief Hadawa'ko, this is Jenny Barnes and her sister, Dawny."

The Chief stepped forward and offered his hand, to which Jenny responded in kind. If she felt fear she did not show it. The Chief, who had lived in concert with white men for many years, spoke fluently.

"I am pleased to meet you, Jenny," he said. His voice was soft, but rich, and vibrated as though all the life energy of the forest flowed through it.

Jenny's hand tingled as he touched her and she was uncertain of how to address such an important figure. Instead, she shook her head dumbly, in unison with their coupled hands.

Hadawa'ko issued a throaty chuckle and responded, "It's all right, Jenny. I come in peace." He looked utterly amused by his own joke.

"I wanna touch him too," said Dawny as she pushed to the forefront and snatched the Chief's hand. "Where'd you come from, Mister? I didn't see you comin'"

"I live just over there," he pointed, "among my brothers in the woods."

"Are there more of you out there?" she asked scouring the line of trees. "Can I see?" Seeing no one, she turned her attention back to the Chief, appraising him no small amount of doubt. "Did your Mommy fix your hair? Cuz I could probably fix it better for you, if you wanted."

Emma laughed and said, "Oh, Jenny, she's adorable!"

"What?" Dawny asked, frowning. "What'd I say?"

"Today, you will see much," Hadawa'ko said, "If you will come with me."

"But where you takin' us, Mister? Is Jenny gonna come too? Cuz if Jenny ain't comin', I ain't comin' either."

Jenny also looked more than doubtful.

"It's perfectly safe!" Emma chimed in. "Do come, Jenny."

"I don't know...after the last time—"

"Oh, him." Emma shivered as she remembered the day in the cellar. "I do admit I find him more than a bit distasteful. You must try and avoid him at all costs. It is safe though, with Chief Hadawa'ko."

"C'mon, Jenny! Let's go and see," pleaded Dawny. "It'll be a lot funner than working in this dumb garden."

"Dawny, do you know what will happen if Daddy catches us not working? Do you know what he'll do if he catches us gone?"

"Well, we'll just go for a minute or two. We won't be gone too long, will we Chief?"

The Chief seemed to ponder this for a moment. "I do not know. Time passes differently on this side," he said. "The journey is not long, yet many moons may come and go before we return."

"Oh, do come!" cried Emma. "We'll have ever so much fun!"

And in the end, Jenny gave in. The world grew silent save for the solitary cry of a Heron as the four stepped through the corn-row leading to the forest.

CHAPTER TEN

Morning trudged steadily towards afternoon as Ruthy and Adam worked. They had long since abandoned the game as the tedious nature of the job crept in and dictated their mood. They had progressed to the far left hand, front corner of the white building. Sweat ran off Adam's forehead and stung his eyes. And still the sun burned down upon them leaving them breathless and red in the face.

Adam lay down his brush and mopped his forehead. "I'm going to the house for a drink," he said. "Want to come?"

"Nah, I'd better stay here," Ruthy answered. "Daddy's liable to be checking in any time. Bring me back some water?"

"You got it, Kid."

Pride welled up in Ruthy as she watched his lengthy strides up the hill and towards the rambling house. To think that someone like him could love her, could love Ruthy Barnes! Having him here this summer had made all the difference. Things were so much better when he was near. And soon, summer would draw to a close and they would leave this place, and leave behind all of this dirty work and the tired feeling that went with it.

"What the hell are you looking at?" Charles demanded rounding the corner. His eyes narrowed as they re-traced the path of her gaze and lit upon Adam just entering the house. "Oh, I see--the hippy boy."

"We're almost done with the front," she offered, hoping to change the subject.

"When he gets back, tell him to get a haircut if he wants to work for me. I won't have no long-haired hippies working on my farm, I'll tell you that right now."

"Okay, I'll tell him."

"And don't you go gettin' no high falutin' ideas in that head of yours, Ruth Ann. You don't need nothin' from the likes of him. He's just here to work and that's just for the summer, got it? When the hayin's done he goes right back to where he come from."

"Sure, Daddy, I wasn't thinkin' anything else."

"Yeah, and I was born friggin' yesterday too," he scoffed. Charles looked hard into Ruthy's eyes, as if he could see her thoughts. "I know what you two are up to, and you don't even need to think I ain't got my eyes on you."

Again, hoping to avoid this discussion, Ruthy bent and dipped her brush back into the bucket of soapy water. As she did this, the silver chain slipped from under her shirt glinting in the bright sunlight.

"Whoa there," Charles exclaimed and let out a sharp whistle. "Whatcha got there, Ruth Ann?"

"What? This?" she asked as she stood back up and tucked the arrowhead safely back inside her shirt. "It's nothin'. Just a necklace. I got it for my birthday."

Charles walked toward her, hand outstretched as he demanded, "Lemme see that. I don't recall seein' nothin' like that on your birthday."

He reached for the chain and tugged the arrowhead back out of its hiding place.

"I didn't get it *on* my birthday," Ruthy answered. "Jenny found it somewhere and she gave it to me, but it was after—"

"Wait just a god-damned minute," Charles said, turning the pendant over in his hands. "That's a real arrowhead. And it's a beauty too. And you say Jenny found it? Where?"

"I don't know, Daddy. I didn't really ask—"

"Well don't that beat all? The little shit finds an arrowhead on my farm and she hands it right over to you! Well ain't you the queen of the goddamned world!"

Ruthy was nervous now. She hadn't seen this coming. "I didn't think—"

"I'll just bet you didn't think when the two of you were stealing my property," he growled. "Do you have any idea what this thing is probably worth?"

"I don't know, Daddy."

"Yeah, you didn't have no idea, cuz you ain't seen me collectin' arrowheads all these years, have you?" His voice was thick with sarcasm and headed straight for anger.

Ruthy didn't know how to answer this last. Would that the ground would open up and swallow her whole...

"That little shit! I'll beat her ass and yours too!" Charles fumed. "Stealin' from me--" With that he gave a yank and snapped the chain off of Ruthy's neck. "I'll be takin' this now, you little thief." The treasured pendant disappeared into his hip pocket.

"But, Daddy, that's mine!" She protested. Her neck burned where the chain had scratched her on its way to Charles' pocket.

"LIAR! Never was, never will be. It come off'n my farm and it damned well belongs to me."

Tears of frustration welled up and out of the girl's eyes. "But...but—"

"BUT NOTHIN'," he screamed. "YOU THINK YOU'RE GONNA GIVE ME A HARD TIME ABOUT THIS? YOU THINK THEM TEARS ARE GONNA GET YOU ANYWHERE WITH ME?"

Charles snatched a bunch of hair from the top of Ruthy's head in the fingers of his right hand and pulled her face into his.

"WELL, YOU GOT ANOTHER THINK COMIN'! NOW QUIT THE GOD-DAMNED

189

CRYIN' OR I'LL GIVE YOU SOMETHIN' TO CRY ABOUT."

With that he shoved hard knocking her to the ground. He began again, slowly this time, as if she were dim-witted, "Now you get your lazy, son-of-a-bitchin' ass back up and get back to work, Girl, before I knock you into the middle of next week."

Speechless, Ruthy didn't move.

"DOUBLE-TIME!" he screamed.

Ruthy picked herself up and brushed away the dirt that was clinging to her wet legs. Refusing to look at him, she dipped the brush once again and began scrubbing angrily at an imaginary spot on the wall.

Charles took one big step forward, threatening to close the gap between them once again. His arm was raised, hand poised to strike. The words he uttered were spoken coldly and clearly, and Ruthy froze as his voice went through her.

"You want another taste, Girl? Huh? Cuz I got plenty more if you need it."

"No, Sir," she answered and resumed scrubbing, although much gentler now and still not looking into his face. *Just a few more weeks*, she thought.

"That's about what I figgered," Charles said and turned to walk away. "Now lemme go find that sister of yours and see where the hell she found this thing. There might be more where this come from."

***

Jesus Christ, Almighty, Charles thought as he headed up the hill for the garden. *I can't trust these goddamned kids for a minute.*

Oh, he knew they were lazy all right, but he thought he was getting that well in hand. But finding something valuable like this and then hiding it from him? Well that just about took the goddamned cake then, didn't it? And they knew damned well what something like this could mean to him. He could probably sell it for a real chunk of change. Good thing he'd caught them at it when he did or God only knew what would have become of the thing. Christ! It wasn't bad enough that he was trying to run this whole operation damned near all by himself—God knew the bunch of them were not much help. Here he was breaking his goddamned back every single day to put food on the table and wouldn't a goddamned one of them so much as pick up a shovel or a pitchfork if he wasn't right behind them making it happen. Lazy sons-a-bitches! If Annette would quit babying them he might be able to get some work out of them. If they didn't run crying to their mother all the time... He was just about sick and tired of this shit.

Well things are going to change around here, by the Jesus. No more Mr. Nice Guy. I'm done with that. I'm going to learn these sons-a-bitches if it kills me. I'll learn 'em even if it kills them! And I don't give a rat's ass what

Annette says about it. I'm about done with her shit too.

Charles was nearing the garden now, and his eyes scoured the rows for the little girls. He felt, as much as saw their absence, but went the distance just to make sure.

"JENNY? DAWN? WHERE YOU AT, YOU TWO?"

Son-of-a-bitch! He'd kick their little asses to hell and back, that's what he'd do. *When I get hold of those two there'll be hell to pay if they aren't in that garden.*

He began to walk the circumference of the garden looking along each row and calling, "JENNY. WHERE YOU AT? DAWN MARIE?"

Nothing. It didn't take long to realize that the two were not going to be found weeding.

"Hmpfff... Can't trust the sons-a-bitches for a minute. Gotta watch 'em all the time," he mumbled and turned and made for the house.

Within minutes he was standing before his mother in the living room. She was sleeping in the recliner as was her habit and he shook her awake.

"Ma. Ma, you seen the little girls? You seen Jenny and Dawny?"

Momentarily confused, the old woman's eyes widened and then narrowed again as her mind found purchase.

"Huh? No, Son. I thought you had 'em out weedin' the garden."

"Well the little shits ain't out there," he sighed. "Just like 'em to go wanderin' off. Probably off playin' somewhere. Annette's got 'em so spoiled, don't none of 'em do as they're told."

"Spare the rod, spoil the child," Grandma answered. "They must get it from her because you sure didn't act like that when you was comin' up. Your father woulda killed ya."

"Well don't you worry 'bout it none, cuz things are gonna change around here, starting right goddamned now. And when I find those two, I'm gonna tan their hides, but good."

"Did you ask that man in the black suit? I've been seeing him wandering around a lot. I don't know how he ever gets any work done."

"Huh? What man is that, Ma?"

"You know, the new hired man."

"The only new hired man I got is Adam and I just passed him on his way back to the milk-house, so I know he ain't seen 'em."

"Oh. Well I ain't seen 'em either. They'll be back though, soon's their bellies get to talkin' to 'em. It's almost noon. It'll be time for dinner soon." Her eyes fluttered sleepily.

"Dinner? Hell, they ain't gonna be able to sit down for dinner when I'm done with them. And they'll be lucky if they can sit for supper."

But sleep had taken Grandma Barnes once again.

"Women!" Charles said in resignation. "Just about the most useless creatures God ever come up with." Well, he couldn't worry about those two right now, he had work to do, by the Jesus. They'd show up, and when they did…

***

"When Jenny and Dawny didn't show up for dinner, I was worried," Eddie continued. "When they didn't show up for supper I was in a goddamned panic."

CHAPTER ELEVEN

"I knew something was wrong the minute I stepped out of the barn after milking that evening. I was walking up the hill towards the house and felt that familiar shift happening in my head again. But this time it jarred me! One minute I was looking right at that house and everything was fine. And the next minute it felt like someone took hold of both of my ears and yanked my head into a hard right! I know that sounds crazy, but I don't know how else to describe it. It stunned me for a moment. But

197

when I got my bearings back and looked up at that house, Lord help me, I wished I could be *anyplace* but standing right there! The grass on the ground in front of me lay withered and dying. Same thing with the flowers in the beds in front of the house. Their gray faces sagged under some weight I could not see. And the house itself? Even worse. The pink and white shakers that sided the house had all gone over to a dull gray. Hell, the sky above that house wasn't even blue anymore!

"But the weirdest thing...the thing I still can't get over, was the faces in the windows. It only lasted a second, mind you, so I couldn't say anything for sure, but I swear to God that I saw people looking out at me from the upstairs windows. Hell if I know who they were. Never saw them before in my life. But there they were, just staring at me.

"That scared the bejesus out of me and I darned near run off right then and there. Plus, by now, I'd considered the idea that the amount of color left in that picture was a measure of the overall health of the place. Giving that it was now almost completely eaten up with black and white (there was just a sliver of color on the right hand side), I figured that couldn't be good. And then I remembered that Annette and the kids were in there. I *ran* the rest of the way up."

Father Murphy did not know what to say to this. He ended up saying nothing.

"When I got there they were already looking for Jenny and Dawny. Dinner grew cold first and then set hard in pots on the stove as we began the search for the girls. We started with the house itself. We tore that place apart looking for those two. We thought they might just be hiding somewhere. But you know how that goes. Sometimes when you go looking for one thing you end up finding something else entirely. Something you wished you never saw..."

The dowser watched from the second floor
landing as Ruthy Barnes climbed the stairs.
He was standing in the doorway of the room
just at the top of the stairs, although he
doubted she could see him. There were a lot
of things she wasn't seeing, but that didn't
mean they weren't there. *She* wasn't quite
there yet, but her toes were right on the line.
As she drew near to the place in the banister
where the three rails were missing, those same
rails shimmered for a moment, blinked out, and
then came back into existence.

A man, middle aged, pasty skinned and
sickly looking, sat on the thin ledge just in front
of the rails. The man watched Ruthy as well,
slipping a noose around his neck and pulling it
tight as he did so. Grinning weakly, he brought
a pistol up to his temple, cocked it and pulled
the trigger. A look of pained surprise crossed

his face the moment before he fell off the ledge.

Ruthy veered far left on the stair, as if to avoid touching something nasty and hugged the wall for the remaining steps. She behaved much like a blind person would. She could sense the things around her, but could not see them.

As she made the top of the stairs and turned the corner her step quickened. She was right in front of the dowser now.

"Get away from me, you son-of-a-bitch!" she hissed. Justus was amused by this. He didn't consider himself *evil*...just dead. She acted like that was contagious! He followed anyway, as she walked the second floor landing passing three bedrooms on her left.

At the end of the landing, the banister made another right turn and a new set of stairs lay in the deep shadow leading up to the attic. Here, Ruthy's feet stopped and her eyes made the journey up the ten, steep steps to the trap door overhead. It was as if she was paralyzed.

Sighing, she took the first step and then stopped again, white knuckles holding tightly to the banister. She remained there quietly for a moment, not even breathing and he realized that she was listening intently. Two more steps and she stopped again. She took the stairs to the top in just this way, stopping for a bit longer each time, growing more and more tense with each step.

Ruthy heaved the heavy trap door upward on its hinges.

"Leave me alone," she said nervously as she stepped into the attic space. "Please don't get me."

Justus followed.

Initially, the trap door opened up onto a kind of make shift foyer; a hallway of sorts constructed of rough-hewn, wooden slats on both the walls and floors. A length of bare wall on the right led to yet another stairway ascending ten feet up and into a large, domed cupola that was the crown of the house. During daylight hours this was an airy, sunny place, wrapped round three hundred and sixty degrees with elongated, rectangular windows. Dusk, however, was fast approaching and the dim remains of sunlight floated lazily down from above and fell impotently to the floor below.

On Ruthy's left was a series of three, ancient, wooden doors, rugged, wooden bars thrown against, *what*? These types of latches were normally put on the inside of doors in order to keep something out. But in this case, it was all backwards—as if the goal was to keep things in. It was these that made her skin crawl and hair stand on end. A look of immense distaste crossed her face as she gingerly walked past them.

The dowser watched as she checked the cupola first. He saw as though through her eyes, heard through her ears. From her vantage point she could see all over the property. She walked the circular landing, scanning the landscape below for any sign of the girls. There were the cows wandering lazily in the field below. She could see the barn and all of the out-buildings, but nothing moved there. She searched the garden patch as well but there was no sign of the girls. Unable to delay the inevitable any longer, she descended the stairs and returned to the hallway below.

"Jenny?" she called. "Dawny? Are you two up here?"   Silence. She knew instinctively that they were not there.

Ruthy approached the first door, that being farthest from the trap door now. Unfortunately she had lingered overlong in the cupola and the hallway filled with lengthening shadows. It was nearly dark outside and she'd brought no flashlight with her. Justus anticipated problems ahead. He remained just a couple of steps behind her—just outside of her range of feeling him.

Ruthy threw the bar, pushed hard on the door and stood before the darkened room. The smell of the place hit her hard in the face and she staggered backward.

"Ugh," she choked and covered her nose and mouth with one hand. It smelled like a sick-room--all of feces and urine, and of old sweat.

She took a deep breath and entered the room anyway. Her left hand and arm, the one not plugging her nose, was extended straight up above her head in search of the string with which to turn on the single, hanging light-bulb. The string was in the exact center of the room. It was at that very moment that her toes finally crossed the invisible line. When Ruthy pulled the string and the first flash of light flooded that room she saw it all.

The room was littered with what looked like living corpses. In every direction, and completely surrounding her were filthy, gaunt figures sitting and lying on the floor. Heavy iron shackles bound their wrists and ankles to the walls. It would have been difficult to describe them as persons; they'd long since gone over to something else. All eyes were on her. Ruthy froze.

"GET OUT!" screamed a woman (thing) on her left.

The creature rose quickly to its feet and began advancing. It wore a torn dressing gown, which while once white, hung now in yellowed shreds. Long, matted hair stuck to its head and face. Pale gray, heavily wrinkled skin drooped in raggedy, leprous patches over bulging cheekbones. Ruthy could see the whites of its eyes burning with indignation and anger. The thing lurched and the chain clanged loudly in protest as it jerked back to the floor.

"Leave us!" she/it bellowed.

"BITCH!" came a voice from behind her. "I'LL KILL YOU DEAD!"

Ruthy heard the rattle of the chains as another one fought to free itself.

She tried to scream, but her voice had already left the room. What came out of her open mouth was more like a breathless "*gak—!*" Her brain screamed though. It screamed '*RUN*' at the top of its lungs, but her feet were glued to the floor like a fixture.

To her right, and at one o'clock, a tattered woman sat in the corner weeping. Raising her head, she stopped crying momentarily and looked at Ruthy with hopelessly dull eyes.

"I just want to go home," she pleaded. "I miss my babies."

"GET OUT, BITCH!" The voice from behind again.

And then, dead ahead, directly at twelve o'clock, out stepped Randall. No shackles bound him. He was free as a bird.

"Glad ya could make it, Ruthy! We're havin' one hell of a party up here! Can ya stay and play today?" Tipping his head back he laughed heartily. "Get it? Stay? Play? today? I'm a poet and don't know it!"

Again Ruthy tried to scream but to no avail.

"You're pretty," Randall said as he skipped over to her. "In a not-dead kind of a way! You'll come around to that though, in time."

Laughing again, he reached out and stroked her arm. Long, dirty fingernails scraped her bare skin.

"Can I pet you, Rooothhhyyy?"

She cringed as he touched her and her feet finally found their motivation. She began to back towards the door.

"You get away from me," she demanded. "Leave me alone!"

As she backed up, Randall waited patiently in place.

"Awwww, c'mon, Rooothhhy! Stay and play with us!" We're a lot of fun once ya get to know us."

He waved one hand beside his face and shuffled his feet, "Cha, cha, cha!"

Ruthy took one more step backwards and then turned to run, but Randall was quicker. The door slammed shut and the bar outside dropped into place.

"I want my Mommy," a child's voice whined from behind her. "Are you my Mommy?"

"She could be," Randall answered. "We could *make* her your Mommy. She'd be a good one."

Ruthy hit the door at a dead run and began beating at it with both fists.

"Lemme out!" she pleaded. "Lemme go!"

And then the light failed.

Ruthy opened her mouth wide and screamed blue, bloody murder as she flailed helplessly at the door. She could hear

Randall's raggedy breath getting closer to her back.

"Stay with us, Rooothhhy doooo," Randall chortled. "We luuuuvs ya!" His hands were now petting the back of her head and sliding down her back.

And then came a voice from the other side of the door. "For Christ's sake, Ruthy, What the hell is wrong now? Where are you?"

"Daddy?" she cried. "Daddy, help me! I'm locked in."

And in the second before her Daddy opened the door, Randall leaned into her face and slid his cold, sand-papery tongue across her cheek. He *tasted* her!

ffffhhhff, came the sound as he drew a sharp breath. *Ppfffppfff* as the end of his tongue flicked rapidly in and out of his mouth.

"Go ahead then, go on with your ol' Daddy," he whispered. "You'll be baaaaack!"

When the door opened at last Ruthy ran straight past her father and down the stairs.

210

Moments later he found her in the kitchen, in her mother's arms, crying hysterically.

"What the hell is wrong with you, Girl?" he demanded.

"Daddy, I'm scared," she sobbed. "There are people up there! Crazy people! Didn't you see them?"

"Oh for Christ's sake," he answered. "There ain't a goddamned thing up in that attic. I was just up there."

"But I saw them. They--they talked to me."

"You little liar," his eyes narrowed dangerously. "Didn't I say I was just up there? Now how are you gonna tell me there are people up there when I didn't see a goddamned thing? You just got a little spooked and you're too damned cowardly to check the rest of the attic."

"Charles—" Annette began.

"Don't you 'Charles' me," he said glaring at her. "I ain't gonna put up with that shit no more." Returning his gaze to Ruthy, he said,

"Now you get your little ass right back up there and get lookin' for them girls."

"No, Daddy," Ruthy cried and buried her head in Annette's shoulder. "I can't, Daddy. I can't go back up there ever."

"Well, Jesus Christ, don't that beat all!" Charles bellowed. "I guess I gotta do it all by myself just like every other goddamned thing around here" And with that he turned and stomped off toward the stairs.

"But Daddy—" Ruthy protested.

"That's enough, Ruth Ann! I don't wanna hear another goddamned word about it."

What he found up there was nothing.

***

Eddie continued, "When we didn't find Jenny and Dawn in the house, we searched the yard and the barn, and then the outbuildings. We looked in every place that made any sense at all and when that didn't work, we looked in places it wasn't even possible for them to be.

"By ten o'clock we had called the town cop. Deputy Raines wasn't exactly happy about being called out so late at night, but his attitude changed once he saw that the situation was serious.

"By ten thirty the neighbors started to show up. The only thing that we could figure was that they had gone wandering and gotten lost in those woods out there. There was no comfort in that thought either, I can tell you. Anything could happen to two small girls lost in the woods at night!

"We spent the whole night searching the woods under the half moon. There must have been damned near forty of us, all toting flashlights and shotguns, just in case. It was a miserable night, dark and raining like there was no tomorrow. You couldn't see shit out there. Now what you have to understand is that one farm neighbors the next and unlike property lines drawn on a map which serve to chop things up into small, tidy packages, real woods go on forever. They could've been anywhere by then.

"And the woods play tricks on you. You get in there and start chasing a sound or a shadow and before you know it you've got yourself all turned around and you can't even figure out where you are, let alone anybody else.

"By the time five a.m. came and it was time to do the milking, those cows were lined up in the barn and bellering to beat the band. We had to quit looking for the girls to take care of them. Tempers were running short and everyone was on pins and needles. The neighbors filed out, one by one, with promises to return as soon as they could.

"And so it went, for days. All of the extra projects were called off as every man was needed for the search. We quit looking at night though. You couldn't see anything much out there anyways and all we needed was to lose another one of the kids.

"The neighbors began to speculate and the rumors flew. Some said Jenny and Dawny had run away. Some figured they were dead somewhere in the woods. And some went so far as to say that Charles was behind it somehow.

"Annette never gave up hope. She never shed one tear! Instead she watched constantly out the windows for any sign of them in the yard. And you could see her cocking her head, listening for any telltale sound. She demanded absolute silence at all times so that she could hear.

"And you could see something else in her too. The change was subtle--something that sneaked in quicker and quieter than a snake in the grass--but it was there if you were paying attention. It was in her attitude toward Charles. She started nit-picking at him over little things. And there was an edge to her voice that said

215

she might be thinking a lot more than she was saying out loud. The wall between them grew wider every day that the girls weren't found.

"The kids too, were quick to blame Charles. Oh, they didn't come right out and say so, but you could tell by the way they looked at him. The scary part for me was that I *knew* he wasn't responsible, at least not directly. In my heart I knew those girls were as gone as gone could be and I doubted very much that we'd ever see them again.

"At first, Charles took the other kid's new attitudes pretty well. He let them get away with stuff they'd have never gotten away with otherwise. I think he did feel somewhat responsible for what happened. But after a day or two of it, you could see his patience wearing thin.

"'Ed,' he said to me a day or two later down in the milk-house, 'now you know I love my kids and I'd do just about anything to have them back.'

"'I know that, Charles,' I said. I imagined any parent would feel that way.

"'But I'll be a son-of-a-bitch if I'm gonna keep puttin' up with all this shit from Annette and the rest of 'em. I'm about goddamned sick of bein' treated like it's all my fault. I didn't have nothin' to do with them wanderin' off.'

"And that was how he saw it. I was having a hard time just figuring out what to say at a time like this.

"'I swear to Christ,' he said, 'if one more of them gives me the least bit of a hard time about anything, the shit is gonna hit the fan!'

"And he meant it too. Truth be told, I thought the day that those two little girls disappeared from the farm was gonna be the worst day I ever spent on the place. But it wasn't nearly as bad as the day they died there."

Father Murphy's jaw went slack.

CHAPTER TWELVE

"I have to admit that what happened next amused me to no end, although it was a guilty pleasure. It was the third morning that the girls had been missing and there was more than a little tension in the air. We all got up at 4:30 a.m. just like normal, though I doubt anyone had really slept much. Charles had us hired men sitting around the dining room table, already going over the day's chores.

"Grandma Barnes was also sitting there, still half asleep and waiting for her coffee. Ruthy, Callie, Beth, and Bonny were in the kitchen

218

rattling pots and pans when Annette walked out of the bedroom dressed in her work clothes. Now, when I say work clothes, I mean her farm work clothes and not the clothes she normally wore to the store. She hadn't gone in since the girls came up missing.

"I saw the look on Charles face go from all business to all pissed off in an instant as he got up and followed her to the kitchen. We didn't mean to eavesdrop, but honestly we couldn't help it. The kitchen was right next to the dining room. And of course the kids were standing there too.

"'Now, Annette, you ain't plannin' on takin' another day off, are you?' Charles asked. You could tell by the tone of his voice that he was having none of it.

"'What do you mean?' she asked. 'Of course I'm going to take another day off. I'm going to go back out and look for Jenny and Dawny.'

"'No, you ain't. There's plenty of us here to look for them girls. We don't need you hangin' around and gettin' in the way all day,' he says.

"'I'm staying,' she answered, and you could tell by the way she said it that she meant it.

"Now any other man would've heard that in her voice, and backed up a piece, but not Charles. Plus she had just hauled that big, old, cast-iron frying pan out of the cupboard and set it on the stove.

"'By the Jesus, Annette, we can't afford for you to be staying out of work one more day,' he says.

"'I said I'm staying,' she repeated, her back towards him.

"Well that pissed Charles right the hell off and he grabbed her by the nape of her neck and shoved her up against the stove.

"'And I said you're going. Now you get the goddamned breakfast on the table and then you get your ass in the bedroom and get changed for work, and I don't want to hear another goddamned word about it!"

By now, Father Murphy had given up reminding himself that his was a God of love. He hated Charles Barnes and he was glad he was dead. He'd make his own confession later.

Eddie continued, "Now, after he said that, he let her neck go and turned and started walking away like it was the end of the story. But it wasn't the end for Annette and she picked up that cast-iron pan and spun around and brought it down right on the back of his thick head. Knocked him straight to the floor!

"And as he lay there, shocked, she looked him dead in the face and said very calmly, 'Don't you ever touch me or my kids again.' She spoke slowly and her face was deadly serious. 'Because if you ever do,' she went on, 'I'll kill you.'

"For a minute, Charles looked like he didn't know what to say. Neither did the rest of us.

We all just sat there gawking at each other and waiting for the silence to end. Grandma Barnes finally spoke up.

"'Charles,' she said, 'If you let her get away with that—'

"But the second she'd opened her mouth Annette turned on her too.

"'You shut up too, you nosey, old Bitch!'

"She meant it too, standing there all squared off and bowed up like she was begging Grandma Barnes to say something back to her. Grandma Barnes looked dumbfounded.

"'And don't you ever touch my kids again either,' she said. 'All this spare the rod, spoil the child shit is over! Things are gonna change around here, by the Jesus, and I don't want to hear another goddamned word about that!'

"And then she turned on her heels, stepped around Charles who was still on the floor, and went right back to cooking breakfast like nothing ever happened."

Father Murphy couldn't help chuckling at this. Eddie was chuckling too, as he went on.

"Somehow I kept a straight face through all of that, although inside I was happy as a pig in shit! I'd waited years for that woman to come around to seeing things for what they were. And for me, the tiniest seed of hope began to sprout. Later that day, when Charles' clothes were moved up into the apartment where Grandma Barnes lived? Well, that little seed grew ten feet!"

***

Just as old age looks backward and remembers, youth looks forward and dreams of things yet to come. Adam had just finished feeding the calves in the barn and was carrying a bucket of grain out to the bull. Hoping against hope, he imagined that today would be the day that Jenny and Dawny would come home and things would return to normal.

Ruthy had been sullen and withdrawn for days and he was worried about her. She refused to go upstairs at all and had taken to sleeping on the living room sofa. Adam was worried about the rest of the Barnes family as well and he wondered at their ability to go on with all that was happening.

It would be impossible to leave at the end of the summer if things didn't work themselves out. How could they? Well, as soon as I'm done slopping this big boy, I'm gonna go back out and find those girls, he thought. We have to find them today.

He imagined finding them, frightened and hungry, in a clearing in the woods, and bringing them back home to their mother. In his mind, he pictured the elation on all of their faces, the happy reunion... It was a gift he wanted very badly to be able to give.

He began to whistle as he walked. The black and white, Holstein bull watched him approach. If most bulls are big, this one was bigger and though it had been a very long time since the huge animal had been weighed, eighteen hundred pounds would have been a fair guess as to its weight. It measured over six and a half feet at its girth and stood nearly a foot taller at the shoulders than the average man. Long, sharply pointed horns jutted out from either side of its head. An excellent stud, it was the prize of Charles' herd. Its name, quite simply, was Bull. On a good day, Bull was mean. But now, a couple of week's worth into that sweet water and this bull was in a foul temper.

Adam opened the wooden gate and stepped inside the pasture. Deep in thought, he failed to notice the bull's stance. As he walked the few feet to the feed trough, the bull watched him, head down from twenty yards away. The gate swung shut with a *bang*.

Still whistling, Adam bent to pour the grain into the wooden trough. Yesterday's grain lay inside like old news.

That's just weird, Adam thought. *I wonder why he's not eating?*

The water trough, however, was dry. Bull's considerable nostrils flared and his eyes burned into Adam's back. Making a mental note to water the bull, Adam shrugged and started pouring the grain into the trough anyway.

Phffffff, Bull snorted and began to paw at the ground. The whistle died in Adam's throat.

Oh Shit!, he thought.

A look of dread crossed his face and he knew instantly that he was in trouble. His heart froze in his chest and a chill crawled up his spine as he slowly turned his head and looked over his shoulder. Bull had closed the gap between them and was now a mere ten yards away.

Mooooaaahhhh, Bull brayed, pawing the ground again, head lowered, horns to the ready. *Phfffffffff*! The huge animal shook its head from left to right a couple of times, as if to make sure those horns were still there and in good working order. They were.

Hoping against hope, Adam began to back very slowly backward towards the gate, eyes glued to the bull.

MOOOAAAHHHH!

This was as much like a roar as a bellow, and terror overtook Adam, who broke into a dead run for the gate.

But Bull was faster. He closed the distance in seconds and dove at Adam, who leaped to the side. Bull's horns caught him just behind the legs and lifting him up he tossed him high into the air as though he were weightless. Adam flopped to the ground like a rag-doll and the last thing he heard before he lost consciousness was the thundering hooves of the bull running towards him. He had just time enough to scream and then the bull was on him.

"Ahhhhhhhggggkkkk!"

The bull used its massive head like a tool to pin Adam to the ground. There was a sickening crunch as it leaped sideways and its hoof connected with Adam's forearm. Another leap and his leg snapped. Digging its horns underneath him, the bull lifted him up again, flinging his limp, pin-wheeling body into the air. And as he fell back to the earth, the bull attacked again.

Annette, who'd heard the commotion from the barn, was also closing in. She wore a look of profound horror on her face as she ran her fastest. Ruthy and Callie trailed behind her.

"Adam!" Ruthy screamed in terror.

Annette had a rifle in her right hand and as she neared the pasture she stopped, dropped to one knee and leveled the weapon at the bull's head. But there was no clear shot to be had as the two bodies, man and bull, merged into one confusing mass of blood and blurry motion.

"GODDAMNIT, BULL, DROP HIM!" she screamed. "BULL! OVER HERE!"

Ruthy and Callie began waving their arms and jumping up and down in an effort to attract the bull's attention.

"Over here, Bull!" they hollered.

"Over here, you son-of-a-bitch!" Annette shrieked and just as Adam's body flew into the air again, the bull heard her at last. It leaped to the right, narrowly missing Adam this time and rounded on Annette, eyes bulging and enraged, great gawps of snot flinging from its nostrils.

CRACK!

The first shot rang out and caught the beast on the shoulder.

Phhffffffff! It blew.

Bull, who had forgotten all about Adam was running straight for the fence now, straight for Annette and the girls.

CRACK!

Bull stopped short. A spot of bright, red blood appeared in the center of his white forehead and began to spread. He fell as if in slow motion, lowering his massive head first, and then dipping his right shoulder until he collapsed on the ground.

"CALL AN AMBULANCE," Annette screamed. "NOW!"

As Ruthy and Callie ran for the house, Annette stepped cautiously into the pen. She cocked the gun and pumped three more rounds into the bull just in case, but there was no need. The bull was gone.

Running to Adam's side she prayed, "Hold on, Kid. Hold on."

Tears streamed down her face as she took in the grisly sight that was once such a handsome, young man. Both legs jutted out from his body at odd angles. It didn't take a doctor to know that they were broken. And his arm was now badly mangled, with a jagged, bloody bone fragment erupting from the skin.

230

Worse than that was the blood pooling up at his midsection. Tearing her blouse off, she balled it up and rammed it into the gaping wound there. Applying as much pressure as she could, she waited for help to come. She waited and she prayed.

CHAPTER THIRTEEN

Dawny's mood brightened the moment she set foot across the threshold of the magical, northern hardwood forest. In direct contrast to the garden, it was pleasantly cool beneath the hundred-foot tall canopy of Maple, Elm and Oak trees. Rich, loamy soil gave gently underfoot and the foursome walked single-file along an ancient, though well-worn trail through the trees. Chief Hadawa'ko was in the lead, followed by Emma, and then Dawny and Jenny.

Emma chatted ceaselessly as she walked, stopping here and there to pluck sprigs of wild herbs that grew freely along the path. As she did so, she identified the plants for the younger girls, spouting strange sounding names like Wood Sorrel, Purslane and Wild Sarsaparilla.

Far from being a quiet place, the forest was alive with the sounds of squirrel chatter and birdsong. Emma knew each of these by name as well.

"Oh look! There's a Black-Capped Chickadee. Oh! And do you hear that? That's the sound a Whippoorwill makes. And don't you just adore the Red-Breasted Robin?"

"Robins is good birds," Dawny replied. "When you see the Robins, then you know spring is finally here."

"That's right, Dawny. We can tell a lot of things just by watching the birds."

"Yeah, like when the ducks fly south for the winter. They make a really lot of noise and it hurts my ears. Then you know it's gonna snow pretty soon."

"Well, I can see that you've been paying attention, haven't you?" asked Emma.

"I know a lot of things," Dawny answered. "I'm not a baby like everybody thinks."

Jenny remained silent. The mention of Robins brought home an ugly memory for her. In her mind, she saw again the dozens of Robin's nests high in the branches of the Maple trees lining the Barnes' driveway. It had been springtime and she had come out here to listen for the telltale chirping of the new baby birds that were nesting in the trees. She'd been coming for days, excited about the impending arrival of new life on the farm. Just the day before she'd heard the first faint peeps as the baby birds began to hatch.

But that day, as she made her way toward the driveway, she was greeted by an ominous silence. Instead of the happy, musical twitter of birdsong, there, lining the gravel driveway were the bodies of dozens of baby robins lying on the ground in small, featherless, gray heaps. She walked the entire circle, picking up the limp and twisted, broken-necked bodies, gathering them in a well she had created in her blouse, until the pile was so large she could carry no more. And when Annette found her there some time later, she was crying quietly and cradling the baby birds.

"They fell out of the nests, Mommy. Why did their Mommies let them fall? Why didn't they take care of them?"

"Oh, Honey," Annette had explained, "That's not how it happened. That's not it at all. Their Mommies were probably out searching for food to feed them their breakfast. While they were away, Starlings came and threw them out of the nest. Starlings and Robins are natural enemies and they do this to chase the Robins off of the farm."

Jenny hated Starlings, and if she could have, she would have killed them all.

"I hate Starlings," Jenny said.

"Yes, they are a pesky lot," said Emma. "I can't imagine what they might be good for, although Papa says all of God's creatures have a purpose."

"Your Papa is wise," Hadawa'ko chimed in. "The Great Spirit has a use for both the black Starling and the Red Robin."

Dawny, who had no such memories of Starlings, came in firmly on Hadawa'ko's side of the argument. "And plus, Jenny, you shouldn't be hatin'. Don't you member? Mommy said it ain't right to hate *anything*. What did the Starlings ever do to you, anyways?"

"Nothing, I suppose," sighed Jenny.

"Well I love all the birdies. They're good and great! I can fly just like them. Did you know that, Jenny?"

She began flapping her arms in an effort to prove that. Emma also began flapping and the two chirped happily up the path for a bit.

Soon, however, Chief Hadawa'ko slowed and began studying the trees intently. Then, as if he'd seen some invisible sign, he parted the brush and stepped off of the trail and into the denser heart of the forest. The girls followed.

"It's not much farther," he said.

The terrain sloped gently upward through the trees, and went on for as far as the eye could see. At first, the foursome labored through heavy underbrush to take the hill. As they climbed, however, the brush thinned and a subtle magic began to work its way into their ears and eyes and feet. The climbing became easier with each step, until finally it felt as though they were gliding effortlessly up the hill.

Time shed its linear feeling and no one had any sense at all of how much of the stuff had passed by. It was as if it took turns standing

237

still and then speeding up, creating a strange sense of near vertigo.

All sound became muted and dreamy, almost as if they were underwater. The sharp call of the whippoorwill softened into a lullaby.

The bright green hues of the forest softened also and took on a pale, blue quality. Sunlight waned and made way for twilight as they broke through to a small clearing. The trees themselves seemed to fade in and out, playing peek-a-boo with the darkening sky.

"I like this place," Dawny said in wide-eyed wonder. "It feels good here."

And it was true, Jenny realized, as she was no longer hungry, hot or tired. She felt just plain happy.

The elevated clearing was no more than a grassy circle roughly a couple of hundred feet in diameter. At first glance, it appeared empty and deserted, surrounded by a dense line of trees. However, even the eyeless, blue-green giants could see the sacred magic of the place, and they reached their limbs in toward its center as if making an effort to scoop some of it up for themselves. And just as the trees popped in and out of shimmery existence, other things began to appear as well.

At the clearing's center, a shy flicker evolved into a head-high, roaring, council fire. As the girls watched, an Indian brave stepped out of the fire, followed by another and then another, each shadowy figure taking a seat on the ground around the fire.

Jenny reached to her side and took Dawny's hand.

"Awwwkkkk!" both girls cried in unison and let go as a strong vibration coursed through their palms.

"You tickle, Jenny!" Dawny giggled.

"It's a very spiritual place," explained Emma. "What you're feeling is each other's energy. You can't feel it out there," she pointed to the edge of the tree-line, "but it's there on that side too. In here though, you can feel *everything*."

"Let's do it again!" cried Dawny and grabbed Jenny's hand, holding on this time. "It feels funny!"

"Every living thing has a vibration," Emma continued. "It's the *spirit* of the thing. Here...feel these leaves." She reached to her side and tugged on the branch of a bush, pulling its greenery toward Dawny and Jenny.

What Jenny felt as she touched the leaves was a soft pulse entering her body through her hand and traveling rapidly through her muscles. She could hear it as well as feel it, and it created a pleasant humming sensation in her mind. She closed her eyes and the whole world became the color green.

Dawny let go of the leaves and began to giggle, and then to laugh. She began running around touching every tree and bush, squealing with delight, until she finally fell to the ground in breathless hysterics. The natives sitting around the fire were pointing at Dawny and laughing as well.

"This is the funnest place I ever been to!" she cried in between whoops. "Jenny, ain't you glad we came now?"

"Is this Heaven?" a wide-eyed Jenny asked Chief Hadawa'ko.

"Not Heaven. The Great Beyond lies through the fire," he answered.

"Oh, and wait till you see it!" Emma said.

"Emma—" the Chief cautioned.

"This is a kind of portal, Dawny," explained Emma. "It's like a doorway."

"Are we going to Heaven, Mister?" Dawny said apprehensively, "Cuz that might not be all right with me. My Grandpa went there and he never came back."

"Don't you worry, Little Bird," Chief Hadawa'ko answered, holding out his hand and helping Dawny to her feet. "I will bring you home safe and sound."

Just then, a wizened, old man leaped out of the fire. He was dressed in ceremonial garb and although his face spoke of his many years, his body was spry and belied his age. The others rose immediately and greeted him with grunts and cries of joy.

"Whoa," Dawny said tugging on Hadawa'ko's loincloth. "Mister, is he God?"

Hadawa'ko chuckled. "No, Little Bird, he is not The Great Spirit. He is Ongwaterohiathe, the Keeper of the Light."

"Huh? The Keeper of the Light? What's that?"

"Do not be afraid. He will not harm you."

From the fireside, Ongwaterohiathe looked briefly in the direction of the children, and then turned and threw a handful of tobacco into the flames. Sparks flew for just a second and then the flames began to grow. Long tendrils of fire stretched upward, towards the heavens like molten lava, curling around one another, intertwining, and then becoming solidified. In fact, it was as though the appearance of the old man solidified everything in and around the clearing, and all of the elements were locked in.

As the girls watched, the flames formed a lofty structure--a tower of sorts--although the thing still glowed red with heat. At its apex, the fire burned white-hot, effectively turning it into a Native American version of a lighthouse. Having done with it, the Keeper turned and made for Hadawa'ko and the girls.

"He is ready," Hadawa'ko said. Let us go to him."

The old man met them half way.

"Why do you bring them?" he asked, gesturing toward Jenny and Dawny. "They should not have come here."

The words that he spoke were not in English, and although they sounded more like grunts to Jenny, than words, she found that she understood them perfectly.

"Ongwaterohiathe," Hadawa'ko addressed him. "Light Keeper. I seek your council tonight."

The sound of a drumbeat commenced from near the tower's edge and was soon joined by that of a rattle. This was constructed out of a tortoise shell filled with small pebbles and dried beans. The natives began to circle the lighthouse, strutting slowly and singing in their native tongue. They sang in unison, softly and slowly and Jenny knew instinctively that this was a prayer of thanks to the Great Spirit.

The Light Keeper reached out and touched Dawny's hair. Then bringing his hand down to lift her chin, he gazed kindly into her eyes and stood silently for a moment. Without shifting his gaze, he answered, "I will give what council I can. Let the children dance."

Emma took both Jenny and Dawny by the hands and led them into the ceremonial circle. They caught on very quickly and were soon mimicking the stomp dance of the natives with

244

glee. Arms at the side, two small steps forward and one back...

Hadawa'ko and Ongwaterohiathe settled on the ground some thirty yards from the dancing. From the surrounding forest, stray souls began to wander in and join the circle.

"Why do you bring them here?" the Light Keeper repeated.

"These are the children who walk where we once walked," Hadawa'ko began.

"I know their faces," the Light Keeper responded. "They have come too soon."

"They are young but the way has been long for them," Hadawa'ko went on, "long and full of trials."

"I know their story."

"They are the children of our people," pleaded Hadawa'ko. "In another time, their mothers and fathers sat as heads at our council fires. But the blood became mixed with that of the white man and they have not been taught our ways. They do not know! Their

245

spirits grow weak even now and I am afraid for
them. Their father—"

"They must walk the path that The Great
Spirit has set out for them. You must not try to
change their course." warned
Ongwaterohiathe. His tone became severe.
"They belong to the white man now."

"I thought only to heal them, Father,"
Hadawa'ko said. "If you would give them
medicine then I will return them to their
people."

The old man considered for a moment.

"This I will do," he answered. "But there is
more that you would ask of me. Speak the
truth as Eagle does, and Bear. Let your words
fly straight, like the arrow."

Hadawa'ko bowed his head momentarily.
In the distance, thunder rumbled as the other
world was pelted by the storm. But here in the
portal, the full moon was high in a clear, starry
sky and when the Chief raised his face again,

the Light Keeper could see the earnest in his eyes.

"Jenny, the dark one," Hadawa'ko began, "dreams each night. Many moons I have watched and it is always the same. She is fearful and cries out like a wounded rabbit."

"Perhaps a rabbit, but a *white* one," Ongwaterohiathe said. "You have no concern in her world."

"She speaks of the broken rainbow!"

Ongwaterohiathe drew a sharp breath. "You are certain of this?"

The Chief shook his head in the affirmative. "I have heard it many times."

Ongwaterohiathe pondered this last for a few moments.

"Orenda speaks to us through the child," he finally answered. "Tonight the Light Keeper will become Dream Walker. I will go with her into the night, and I will look with my own eyes on the broken rainbow. We will see what is to be done."

CHAPTER FOURTEEN

Distant thunder merged with the native drum beat, creating a deep, hypnotic undertone as the girls stomped around the circle. The fire was warm and comforting, but at the same time the sound of the tortoise shell rattle prickled at the base of Jenny's skull. *Tic-a-tic-a-tic*...like the warning rattle of a coiled snake. Her mind was peaceful, but clear and alert, and as she brought first one foot down, and then the other, she focused on stepping in exactly the same place as the native before her had. And each time her foot sank into the empty footfall it was rewarded with the soothing pulsation that he left behind.

She no longer felt like a child. She was wide awake for the first time in her life, and the colors that made up her being ran and mixed with the red and gold of the fire and the deep blue of the big sky above.

The native chant rang out clearly and as crisply as the air around them.

Hai...haihhaih,
When women dance,
Their feet never leave the ground.
Hai...haihhaih,
They are life-givers like Grandmother Moon
And our Mother, the Earth...

Chief Hadawa'ko stepped into the circle behind her and the march continued. The Light Keeper, however, stood just to the outside of the circle as if in readiness. In his right hand, he held a wooden mask; the mask of the False Face Society. It was the mask of a healer.

The mask itself, bordered on hideous. Carved from indigenous Maple, it had been stained a very dark brown. The face, although human in nature, was grotesquely distorted. Bulbous, white eyeballs glared from within bony, withered cheeks, and a long, hooked nose sat between them. The lips, thin and elongated, spread into a malevolent grin, tongue lolling out and to one side. Course, black hair, was parted in the middle and cascaded down either side.

As Ongwaterohiathe tied the mask to his face, the chanting subsided. Native Americans: braves, warriors and squaws alike, stepped well back and immediately dropped to the ground, seating themselves once again around the fire. Emma stepped back as well, but as Jenny and Dawny made to follow her, the Light Keeper stopped them.

"You must stay with them," he said and indicated the band of stray souls left standing in the circle.

These were the raggedy band of some twenty people that had stepped out of the treeline at the edge of the clearing and made their way into the dance. They appeared to be a mixed lot, none of them Indian, though some were old, some young, some were men, some women, and all seemed a bit confused as to why they were here and what they were to do next. They shuffled aimlessly about and whispered amongst each other while they waited.

"Father—" Hadawa'ko protested.

"Still your tongue!" Ongwaterohiathe hissed. "Does the squirrel teach the Eagle how to fly?"

Hadawa'ko lowered his head and remained silent. Jenny held tightly to Dawny's hand now.

To Emma, she whispered, "But I'm scared."

"You must be brave, both of you," Emma commanded. "You're becoming a part of the tribe now. Tonight you'll be asked to join the Haudenosaunee."

"I want to go home," Dawny pleaded. "I miss my Mommy now."

"Do you know what courage means?" asked Emma. "If a person goes into battle unafraid, then he is not brave. He is merely foolish. It is the warrior who is terribly afraid, but goes on in spite of it, who is truly courageous. Have faith!"

Indeed, both girls were terribly afraid, but they held their ground and as the drum-beat began again they joined the others in a new, smaller circle. Once again, arms to the sides, two steps forward and one back, they began the march back toward the beginning.

The Light Keeper did not join the circle. Instead he began to step slowly, in the opposite direction from the others, and in a larger circle outside of them. As he advanced, his shadow grew taller, and before long he became as a giant to the other dancers. The chanting resumed, and his step quickened. He began to leap and stamp the ground violently, leaping again and turning about. As he did so, he shouted and cried out with sharp, guttural squeals. His arms deftly wielded imaginary weapons and he stabbed and cut the air randomly in an effort to frighten evil spirits away.

Afraid to do anything other, Jenny remained obediently in the circle, stepping along it seemed, towards some frightfully unknown end. An elderly woman, directly counter to her, shuffled arthritically along.

Anin...yadeyho... the braves chanted.
The Great Spirit waits by the fire
On the other side and we must be ready.

"We must be ready," the old woman said, and straightened up.

In front of her, a broken and bruised man on crutches dragged one twisted leg behind him, digging a small trench as he went.

Step, drag, step, drag, back...

253

Pure of heart and strong in spirit,
We are ready.
On the backs of eagles,
To the sky world we fly.

"We are ready," Twisted Leg said, and pulling his injured leg back around, he tossed the crutches lightly to the side and began to walk normally again.

Step, step, back, step, step, back...and the masked Keeper circled.

The Maker waits and we are ready,
No evil follows us to the Great beyond.

"No evil," said a tearful child across the circle, "we are ready." And the child smiled.

Thrice around the circle and several minutes later, Ongwaterohiathe shrieked and stopped suddenly.

Pure of heart and strong in spirit,
We are ready...

"We are ready," repeated every member of the raggedy group, each and every one of them whole again. Every member save Jenny and Dawny, who were not ready, though bravely they lingered.

"We are ready," the Keeper said. "It is time."

And with that, both the chanting and the drum cadence stopped. The night itself, held its breath as Ongwaterohiathe stepped through a break in the circle and stood before the council fire. He reached his hand out towards Twisted Leg. Twisted Leg took it gleefully, and the Light Keeper leaped back into the fire pulling the man in with him. A murmur of appreciation went through the crowd.

"Awwww, no," said Jenny sadly. "We ain't ready." Once again she grasped Dawny's tingly hand.

"No way," said Dawny looking uncertainly at Chief Hadawa'ko. "Mister? Mister, you promised." Hadawa'ko remained silent, staring straight ahead as the fire burned high and hot behind her.

"Have faith!" mouthed Emma and held one hand out toward the girls, fingers crossed.

The Light Keeper leaped back out of the fire and held his hand out once more. The old woman stepped up, took it, and followed him into the fire.

Old Woman was followed by a previously emaciated, old man, and so on. One by one, the dancers followed the Light Keeper into the flames until only Jenny and Dawny and the once crying child were left.

Once more Ongwaterohiathe leapt from the flames back into the clearing. Crying Child stepped up and took his hand, but before she turned to face the fire, she spoke up.

"See you soon," she said sweetly, as she waved and was whisked away as well.

"I'm sorry I made you come, Jenny," Dawny said through her own tears. "I wish we'd stayed in the stupid garden now."

"Don't worry," Jenny said. "I got you, Dawny." She sounded a great deal more sure of that than she felt.

"And Grandpa will be there, won't he? When we get to heaven? Will he know that we are Haudenosaunee now?"

"I don't know, Dawny."

"It's very hard bein' an Indian, isn't it, Jenny?"

Jenny swallowed.

Ongwaterohiathe returned.

"Uh oh," said Dawny. "Are you ready, Jenny? I think it's our turn now."

As the Light Keeper reached out, Jenny, still holding tightly to Dawny's small hand, stepped up. Dawny turned once more towards Chief Hadawa'ko.

"Tell my Mommy I love her," she said. "Please, Mister?"

Hadawa'ko gave no answer, but continued to stare straight ahead.

As the Light Keeper drew the girls to him, he knelt on one knee and removed the mask.

"You are brave beyond counting," he said gazing intently into their faces. "Your hearts are true, and your spirits are once again made strong."

Emma looked nervous now, but Chief Hadawa'ko remained stony-faced.

Ongwaterohiathe continued, "But you are right. You are not ready. You must return to your father and to your mother."

Jenny's face crumpled with relief.

"Did you hear that, Dawny? We don't have to go!"

"Really? Oh, that is good and great! Can we go home now, Mister? Can we go home, Keeper?"

From amongst the braves, Emma beamed. "You've passed the test! Jenny, Dawny, you've passed with flying colors!"

Hadawa'ko closed his eyes tightly for a moment, reigning in the raw emotion, and then let out a huge sigh.

"I'll take you back in the morning, Little Bird," he answered, "when the sun lights our way."

Dawny ran to him, throwing her arms round his neck.

"You did keep your promise, then, didn't you, Mister? You did keep it!"

The remaining Native Americans rose now, to their feet and one by one they leaped into the council fire, returning from whence they came. Ongwaterohiathe did not follow.

Jenny had assumed incorrectly that his business there had concluded for the night. Instead, he and Hadawa'ko readied make-shift pallets out of Indian blankets for the girls to sleep on. It was late, and the journey tomorrow would be a long one. The pallets were removed by some distance from the fire and the girls snuggled happily together under the warm blankets.

Hadawa'ko and Ongwaterohiathe busied themselves nearer the fire, throwing tobacco on it and pleading with Orenda to bring forth the pitcher of dreams and pour it out on them from the heavens above. They would have only this one magical moon with which to walk through them.

"That was some night!" Dawny said sleepily.

"Yeah, except some of it was scary," Jenny answered.

"I know. Hey, Jenny?"

"Yeah?"

"Ya member when the people was comin' out of the trees?"

"Yes."

"Member? They was comin' out and comin' into the dancin'?"

"Yeah," Jenny was tentative now.

"Well I thought for just one minute that I saw Adam there too. I really thought I saw him. And then he just disappeared again."

"You saw him too?" Jenny asked. "I thought I was imagining things."

And indeed, two towns and one whole dimension away, Adam Morris slipped quietly in and out of death.

CHAPTER FIFTEEN

In a sparse hospital room, in the small city of Walpole, about thirty miles north of Southtown, Ruthy Barnes sat and watched Adam Morris cling tentatively to life. As he drifted in and out of consciousness, he muttered unintelligible and disjointed phrases. At first, hearing him mention Jenny and Dawny brought her great hope, but when he added something about Indians she attributed it to the serious concussion he suffered from.

The surgeon, who had painstakingly pieced Adam back together, had given the Morris family a very hopeful prognosis. In addition to the concussion, Adam suffered from a ruptured spleen, which had promptly been removed, a good bit of minor internal trauma, which he'd repaired, and of course, several broken bones. He'd been in surgery for most of the night, but Doctor Phillips emerged from the operating room early this morning and announced that without further complications, Adam should make a full recovery.

Far from being all right, however, Adam's recovery would take a good deal of time. There would be several more surgeries later on, to reconstruct the mangled bones of his arm, and both legs had still to be casted. He was lying flat on his back now, heavily dosed with Morphine. The Orthopedic Doctor would be in shortly to assess the damage to his arm and attend to the casting of his legs.

Sitting here, watching Adam being broken, felt so damned surreal to Ruthy. Normally, at this time of day, she would still be at home doing her chores. She might be fighting with one of her sisters, or getting the business from Charles, but regardless, she would be knee deep in the proposition of cleaning up something unpleasant that the animals had left behind. And as annoying as that always had been for her, it paled in comparison to the desperation she felt now.

And somehow, she knew that this was all her fault. Adam wouldn't be here at all if it weren't for her. Instead, he'd be off somewhere happily tossing a football with his buddies or something. Or maybe if she'd worked harder, instead of taking advantage of the extra help...Well, it should have been her in there feeding Bull yesterday morning, shouldn't it have? And that thought was no consolation either.

Adam stirred, and mumbled something about fire, startling her out of her contemplation. There was only one thing for it, and that was to pray. Ruthy approached the side of Adam's hospital bed and got down on her knees.

Folding her palms together, she began, "Dear God...I know that I ain't worth a whole lot, and you sure don't owe me nothin'. But God, Adam is a good person and he doesn't deserve this. So if you could help him get better, I'll do whatever you want. I promise from now on, I'll do my own chores and do 'em right. I'll do whatever Daddy wants me to without complaining. And I won't make him mad anymore.

And God, if you need to take someone, please take me. I don't know how you'll do it, and hopefully it won't hurt too much, but if somebody's got to go, better it be me than anybody else.

So please, God, and Jesus, I'm askin' you—no, I'm *begging* you—please don't take Adam away."

Ruthy continued to pray, and pray her hardest, right up to the moment the Doctor came into the room. She made deals with God, and Jesus, and every religious figure her tired mind could call up. And by the time she was done, she'd racked up a considerable amount of holy debt. This was debt she may full well spend the balance of her life trying to repay.

But Adam was allowed to go on.

CHAPTER SIXTEEN

Ongwaterohiathe felt ill at ease the
moment he stepped onto the darkened forest
pathway that was Jenny's dream plane. He
sensed that Jenny wasn't far ahead of him, but
there were others here too, and the air was
heavy, the malevolence having set in long ago.
It felt almost greasy and stuck to his skin and
hair. Likewise, it no longer smelled fresh, but
old somehow, like something that has been
packed away for a very long while in an airless,
black trunk.

The Dream Walker no longer walked on two legs, but rather four as he had assumed the form of his spirit guide, the clever Red Fox. The dream led him along the same path that the children walked earlier to get to the portal but it was now grown over with thorny brambles and thick, twisted brush and the going was difficult. The forest itself was eerily silent although the light of the moon reflected off several pairs of eyes as its inhabitants came to investigate his passing. These he did not fear. Deer, Bear and Raccoon were his brothers.

Working his way under and around the tangle of brush, he progressed deeper into the forest. Intuition told him that Jenny would follow the path, but he stopped frequently, sniffing the ground in order to pick up her scent. Various scents lay one on top of the next in neat layers and Jenny's was somewhere near the top. It read to his keen nose as if several had gone before her, but at least one had followed behind. It was the scent of this last that he didn't like. He didn't like it at all. Ongwaterohiathe knew that the dream plane, as part of the larger spiritual world, held many kinds of dangers, even for an observer such as himself. In the world of the living, the worst thing that could happen was death. Not so, here. Stopping, he sat and threw back his head in order to sniff the air. A new smell wafted in on the night breeze. Blood. Fresh meat! He made the smell as being just ahead and walked on with renewed caution.

A few feet more and he saw the reason for the tang. An iron contraption sat in the middle of the pathway, a dead rabbit lying between its gaping jaws. He recognized it instantly as a bear trap. Hunger was, however, the bane of the living, and of little consequence to him. He'd lost his taste for blood long ago. Still, he was curious and sniffed gingerly just at the edge of the thing. His nostrils caught the vague smell of sulfur. It was as he thought then, a trap set by the other, the one with the bad smell. *Was the trap meant to catch him*? Circling around it, he continued on.

After a short while, he came to the place where the path veered off and he would have to leave it to ascend to the clearing. Jenny's scent was strong and he knew that she had been here only moments ago, but the way was blocked to him. A rough-hewn, wooden fence had been thrown up across the path. At its center, stood a gate and the words **KEEP OUT OR DIE!** had been scrawled across it. A large, rusty padlock was threaded through the hasp. He would have to find another way in.

Scurrying along the fence-line he prayed silently to the Great Spirit to help him find that way. In his mind, a subtle picture began to form. He envisioned a pile of boulders next to the fence, and he knew that they'd be waiting somewhere ahead. The Great Spirit was indeed with him and within moments the boulders appeared. The Dream Walker climbed quickly up the rocks and leaped over the fence, but he'd lost precious time. Picking his way back to the trail, he worried that he would be too late. Night Wind called out to him, whistling through the trees.

Hurry! It cried. *Time does not wait!*

The Dream Walker could not fail his people! He must find the broken rainbow and determine what it meant. Long ago in space and in time, a woman of the Haudenosaunee had dreamt of it. So intense was the dream, that the woman brought its tale to the council fire. The broken rainbow, all agreed, symbolized the breach in relations between Indian and white man. Beyond that, the dream heralded the advent of a great peacemaker; a son who would be born to the woman and would heal the rainbow bringing peace and understanding between the two peoples.

Indeed, all of this had come to pass. For a time, there had been peace. But the white man ever breaks his promises and the red man paid the debt in chits of blood. Perhaps this time it would be different. He had to know!

Picking up the pace he began to run back towards the trail. He ran with fervor, and with great purpose throwing caution to the four winds. Brambles tore at his flesh, and branches swatted him in the face as he passed by. All of these, he ignored.

Suddenly, from somewhere in the bushes to his left, came a low growl. Ongwaterohiathe froze. In that instant he knew he'd made a grave and irreversible error. Every hair on his body stood straight up. One quick sniff told him all he needed to know and he began backing up.

He was too late though as a great rustling of brush immediately gave way to the largest canine he'd ever seen. The beast went well over two hundred pounds, was black as the night and came at him fast, teeth bared through foamy, gaping maw. At once, he recognized the symptoms of rabies. The dog was mad!

The Dream Walker ran.

Hell dog ran faster.

Within seconds the horror was on him and he was down. Struggling valiantly, he twisted and writhed, but was unable to gain his freedom. Pain coursed through his body as the beast's teeth sunk deeply into the back of his neck paralyzing him. As it lifted his body into the air, it began shaking its large head back and forth in an effort to break his neck. Consciousness abandoned him.

When he returned to his senses, he found himself lying on his side at the edge of the clearing, the great dog standing guard above him. Unable to do anything other, he watched the scene before him unfold.

"Awww...too bad, Jenny!" Randall chortled. "Go back four spaces!"

"Too bad, Jenny," Charles parroted. "So sad."

Ongwaterohiathe did not see his native brothers in the clearing, nor did he see the council fire. Instead, a giant wooden platform resembling the playing board of a child's parlor game had been constructed. He had little understanding of such things, though Jenny would recognize it as being very similar to a game called Mousetrap, which she had received at Christmas last year.

Rough squares painted with numbers and letters meandered around its edge. The center of this behemoth was built from scraps of wood hastily nailed together, as if created by a child. Added to these were a number of heavily rusted, metal castaways.

First, standing at about five-feet tall was a crank which turned a pair of gears. Adjoining these, a ten-foot long rod was attached to a horizontal base. At the far end of this, another rod stretched several feet vertically and a six-sided sign rested on it. The word *STOP* was printed on it. In front of that a tall, antique lamp-post had been planted in the earth and Randall was sitting atop this with his long legs and feet dangling. To his left hung a dowel with a boot tied to its bottom end. Resting uneasily to the fore of the boot and on top of a rickety wooden stairway was a bucket. A twisted and bent rain gutter wound its way from the bottom of the stairway towards another rusty metal structure. This was the rough equivalent of a twenty-foot scaffold and housed a wooden deck with a large opening and beneath that, an ancient, yellowing, claw-footed bathtub. The remainder of the contraption was comprised of a diving board, washtub and another twenty-foot pole with a large, open ended cage perched precariously at its apex. The thing looked shaky at best and the various metal parts creaked and groaned as if in warning.

Mark huddled on the diving board, wide eyed and pale. He was dressed only in thin pajamas, and wore a brown plastic holster with one, toy six-shooter on either side. Silver toned, plastic bullets inserted round the belt, gleamed in the moonlight.

Charles, several spaces ahead of Jenny, who was mid-way on the board, had taken on the form of a six-foot rat. Only his face remained his own. He held his own tail in his hands, twisting and wringing it in his excitement.

"That's right, little Jenny," he said. "You got to go on back."

"Don't choo cry little girrrlllll!" laughed Randall from his perch.

Jenny did look as though she were going to cry. She looked frightened half to death. She was also dressed in pajamas and clenched a moldy, pie-shaped hunk of cheese in her hands. She turned and looked wistfully behind her at a smaller, thinner-than-Charles, rat-version of her mother. The Annette-rat sat trembling on the ground directly underneath the cage.

"I'm sorry, Mommy. I didn't do good that time," Jenny said and walked back four spaces. She had to stretch her legs full out in order to make each space.

"My turn," said Charles and picked up a basketball-sized die. He tossed it gaily to the ground where it tumbled for a moment and then landed with the number six face up.

"Six for kicks!" he hollered, sounding oddly like Randall. "And Jenny takes the licks!" He took six rodent hops forward.

"Slick!" Randall shouted with hearty approval. "Your turn again, Jenny Girl. Ain't we havin' fun?"

As if she'd willed it, the die slid eight feet across the board and stopped at Jenny's feet. She retrieved it and gave it a toss. Two. Two small spaces, but at least they were in a forward direction.

"Righty-roo, then," said Randall. "Charles, your go now. Step right up!"

The die slid back to Charles.

"One!" yelled Charles. "Perfect!" and hopped onto the space marked *SAFE*. "One is fun and Jenny's damned near done!" He was a mere two feet away from the Annette-rat and two spaces away from landing on the *TURN CRANK* square.

Randall's eyes sparkled. "All you other mousies better run!" he shouted. "Your go, Jenny!"

Jenny rolled a four. The Annette-rat scurried out from under the cage and started for the edge of the board.

"Ohhhh, noooo!" cried Randall. "No you diddly-eye-don't."

And Annette-rat slid back to her spot beneath the cage.

"We can't have that now, Annette. Little Jenny wouldn't have even stopped to play if you weren't the prize now would she? No sireee, Bob! She'd have kept right on going if her Mommy wasn't in so much trouble. But all work and no play, as they say--"

Annette-rat trembled visibly.

"You again, Charles. Get a good one!"

Charles picked up the die. "Come on baby, Daddy wants a new pair of shoes," he shouted excitedly. The die came up Five.

"Oh no!" shouted Randall. Five spaces took him past *TURN CRANK* and put him right in the middle of the cheese wheel with Annette. "Looks like Charles is in a baaaad waaaay!"

"Hmpff..." Charles scoffed. "She'll never make it to the *TURN CRANK* in time to get me. She'd need a ten for that and that shit just ain't happenin' with a single dice."

He turned to face the Annette rat. "All's I need now's a three and I'll be there. And then you're going to be caught in the rat-trap! That'll learn you. You oughtn't to have been such a bitch!"

Annette recoiled as though she'd been slapped.

Jenny's turn. Four again.

"DOG-BONE SPACE!" Randall shouted gleefully. "Randall's rooole!"

Jenny moved four spaces forward.

"Randall's rule?" questioned Charles. "What in the hell is Randall's rule?"

"Oh, this is goodly," Randall replied. "You're going to love this. Jenny gets to trade in her cheese and switch places with any player on the board."

"Awww, that ain't fair," Charles whined. "Now I'll have to go all the way back. Are you sure that's the way it's supposed to be played?"

"I said *Randall's* rules, Dumbo! It's *my* game and I say how it's played."

Charles looked more than a little unhappy. "Well, at least if she sends me back then she'll be on the cheese stead of me. Then I'll get her and her mother. Kill two rats with one cheese, you could say."

Randall found this hilarious. "Do we have a winner then? What's it gonna beeeee, Jeeennnny?" he hollered.

Jenny carefully laid her piece of cheese on the board. Like the die, it slid across the floor and came to rest near a stack of other cheese pieces off to the side.

"Randall's Rule," said Charles. "She's gonna make the trade."

"I've decided who to trade with," said Jenny.

"Can't wait to hear this," Charles answered sarcastically, "since there's really only two of us playing."

"I'm going to trade with my Mommy."

"Oh ho! That's rich!" laughed Randall. "Out of the mouths of babes..."

"Can she do that? That ain't hardly fair," Charles said.

"Randall's rules," said Randall. "I said she could trade with ennnnnyyyybody."

Annette-rat hopped dutifully to the dog-bone space, passing Jenny on the way. Jenny took her place on the cheese wheel.

"Alrighty, then, my turn now," Charles said. "C'mon lucky number three!" Picking up the die, he blew on it and gave it a mighty heave. The die tumbled across the floor and tottered on the number five.

"Damn!" he shouted, but the die did not rest. It teetered back and forth for a moment and finally toppled over to reveal three dots. "Yipee!"

As the Charles-rat hopped to the *TURN CRANK* space the gears began to spin. Ongwaterohiathe watched in horror as the stop sign engaged the boot, which kicked over the bucket. Spilling out of the bucket, a large silver sphere rolled down the rickety stairway, falling into the rain gutter and making its winding way toward the scaffold. Upon its arrival, it disengaged a pole causing another sphere to roll off the deck and into the bathtub. Slowly, it rolled the length of the tub, dropping through a hole in the bottom, and onto the end of the diving board. Mark shrieked as he was catapulted upwards and into the washtub. Unseated now, the cage began to rock and then to shimmy down the pole. Ongwaterohiathe couldn't watch. As he diverted his eyes he saw something on the other side of the clearing. The broken rainbow! And then darkness took him again.

***

Morning came and Hadawa'ko led his small party back through the woods and toward the farm. As he walked, he tried to put the night's events together again in his mind. All had been quiet for a time. He'd sat for a long while, Jenny sleeping beside him, the Light Keeper sitting cross-legged, deep in prayer. He was certain that Ongwaterohiathe had entered Jenny's dream plane. But when he'd returned

283

from there, he'd had just time enough to issue a quick warning before he'd slumped over and gone comatose.

"Do not...try and save her," the Dream Walker had said, through raggedy, pain-filled breaths. "I saw...the rainbow. But it lies...on the other side of the clearing. On this side, death marks her!"

What had gone wrong in there?

CHAPTER SEVENTEEN

By the time Jenny and Dawny broke through into the garden it had been exactly five days since they'd gone missing. The rain had stopped days ago and the summer sun was hot and high overhead once again. They were sweaty, dirty and more than a little hungry. Charles, who was in the barn at the time, saw them first.

"Well I'll be a Son-of-a-bitch," he said, "look who's back."

And with that, he was out the door and heading up the hill towards the garden. As he walked, he unbuckled his belt and began pulling it from the loops in his pants.

"Jenny!" he hollered. "Dawny! Where in the hubs of hell have you girls been?"

He had every intention of teaching those girls a lesson they'd not soon forget. Annette, however, had been looking out the window and had seen them within seconds as well. She also saw Charles coming up the hill and was determined not to let him get to the girls. She ran out of the house and down the steps.

"Jenny! Dawn! Oh, my babies! Thank God, you're back!" and she rushed to their sides, scooping them up and kissing their faces. "I knew you'd come back! I just knew it!"

Charles arrived just after her.

"What in God's name would ever make you two wander off like that?" Charles demanded. "And where in the hell have you been?"

"We went to see the Indians, Daddy," Dawny answered. "And we had fun, didn't we, Jenny?"

"Bullshit! By the Jesus, I'll tan your little hides!"

"No, you won't, Charles. Not this time," Annette said, and from her tone it was obvious that she meant it. She began walking toward the house, her babies held protectively in her arms.

"These are my goddamned kids, Annette. You ain't gonna tell me how to handle 'em, by the Jesus."

"You were supposed to be watching them, Charles. You and your mother--"

"Well by God, I got a farm to run, don't I?" he answered angrily.

"Yeah? And what's *her* excuse?" Annette shot back. "Maybe watching my kids is interfering with her all day nap?" She set both kids gently down and gave them a gentle push

287

toward the house. "Go on inside, girls, Mommy will be in, in a minute."

Jenny and Dawny ran for the house.

"Ruthy! Callie! Everybody! Wait till you hear what Jenny and I done!" Dawny exclaimed. They were up the steps and in the house in an instant.

Annette turned and faced Charles.

"If you lay one hand on those kids, I am leaving."

"Leaving? Where in the hell do you figure you'd go? Who the hell would have you? You keep it right up, Annette, and within a week those kids are gonna be so spoiled they won't listen to nobody. I guaran-goddamned-tee it."

"Those kids bust their asses around here trying to please you, Charles, and nothing they do is good enough. I've had just about all of that I'm gonna take. Now you just go on back to the barn and run your goddamned farm. You'll have your hands full with that. I'm going to go back in the house and make sure those two kids know how happy I am that they're back home."

And Charles did come back to the barn, but he wasn't happy.

"Fucking Bitch!" he screamed as he slammed through the milk-house door startling one of the barn cats who'd been sitting nearby. The frightened cat darted in front of him in an attempt to get out of his way, tripping him on its way past. Charles fell to his knees on the concrete floor.

"SON-OF-A BITCH!" he screamed in agony. In a split second he found his feet again and grabbed the offending animal. He had it around the waist, in one hand and he brought that hand above his head. In the last second of its life, the cat howled in fear, and then Charles brought his arm down and released the beast, slamming it head first into the cement floor. The cat shuddered, jerked, and then, eyes wide open, moved no more.

"Get that Son-of-a-bitch out of my sight," he barked, and stomped off into the barn.

The girls, in the meantime, were given a hero's welcome; fed, bathed and put straight to bed with hugs all around.

No one believed their fantastic story, of course. It was put down to the overactive imaginations of small children. When the newspaper called that weekend requesting an interview with the children, Charles quickly declined. He was not about to have the entire town thinking that he'd raised a couple of liars.

CHAPTER EIGHTEEN

Charles sulked while the weekend passed and on Monday Annette reluctantly returned to work. She had asked if she might work overtime to help make up for the week she'd lost and that request had been granted. She'd be working double shifts for the entire week and the person who'd filled in for her last week would have the time off. That meant she'd get home late every evening.

Grandma Barnes was once again entrusted with the care and feeding of Jenny and Dawny, but after having been upbraided for allowing them to get lost, she was in a bit of a snit. They sat now, in the living room, in front of her chair, coloring in their coloring books.

"Now, that your mother's gone I'll let the both of you in on a little secret," she huffed. "It's gonna be a good, long time before either of you gets to see the light of day again. You're going to sit right here, inside of this house with me, *every* day for the *rest* of the summer."

Jenny and Dawny said nothing.

"Do you hear me? Say?"

"That will be good with me," Dawny answered. "I like staying in here with you."

Jenny searched her face for the lie. Smiling, Dawny brought her crossed fingers out from behind her back, and just enough to her side that Jenny could see them, though Grandma was none the wiser.

"Hmmpff, we'll see how happy you are after a few days stuck in here with me. At least I'll

know you're not going to wander off again."
Her crocheting needles were flying today.

"Can we watch T.V., Grandma?"

Grandma Barnes screwed up her face in preparation for another tirade. Just as she was about to open her mouth to speak, a look of complete and utter confusion crossed her face. She closed her mouth briefly, thought for a moment, opened her mouth once again, and then lapsed into momentary silence. Slowly, clarity returned and she began to smile first and then to grin.

"Wouldn't you rather go out into the side yard and play hopscotch?"

Grandma actually giggled!

"Huh?" Jenny and Dawny looked at one another with amazement.

"Papa says that children require an extra dose of sunshine and laughter in order to grow up properly."

"Emma!" Jenny shrieked.

Dawny was amazed. She rose to her feet immediately and climbed into her grandmother's lap. Putting one small palm on each of her grandmother's cheeks she pulled on Grandma's eyelids until they were opened wide. She drew her own face as close to Grandma's as she possibly could, and narrowing her eyes she peered inside.

"How in heck did you get inside of Grandma?" she asked. "I don't see you in there, but it must be you! Now, that is one good trick."

"I can't explain it exactly," Grandma/Emma replied. "It's just easier with her for some reason. Papa showed me how."

"Well, where in the heck did Grandma go then?" Dawny asked. "Is she in there too?"

"Yes, she's here, but it's like she's sleeping. So, would you like to get outside for a bit? I can only stay for a while and then you'll have your grandmother back."

And, indeed, the three had a grand time playing hopscotch for the next hour, though Emma's playing ability was somewhat compromised by having to force Grandma's ancient and long-sedentary muscles into action.

By the time Charles slammed through the front door looking for lunch, they were back inside, crayons and coloring books splayed out in front of them once again. While Jenny and Dawny sat cross-legged, it seemed that 'Grandma' had lost all sense of modesty and propriety. She was lying flat on her stomach in her dress, apron and heels, red crayon happily in hand, with one knee bent, leg and foot pointing towards heaven.

"Ma! Is lunch ready yet?" Charles demanded.

Grandma looked startled and then confusion set in again. She was silent for just a moment.

"Ma? What in the hubs of hell are you doing on the floor? Have you lost your goddamned mind?"

"I was just telling the girls they were grounded for the summer," she said weakly. She looked at the crayon in her hand as though it were a serpent, and quickly threw it into the pile. "I don't know how I got down here."

"Yeah," Charles snapped. "It looks like that's what you were doing."

"Owwww," she groaned as her muscles protested. "Help me up, Charles."

"For the love of Christ, Ma, do I need to hire someone to watch you too now?" Charles huffed as he rolled her over and unceremoniously lugged her up and back into her chair. "And where the hell is lunch?"

"I, uh...good Lord! The time must've gotten away from me. Seems like we just had breakfast. I'll get after it right away."

"Aww, damn!" Charles said.

Through the window he saw a car entering the lower driveway by the milk-house. He walked over to the window and peered out, shielding his eyes from the bright sunlight with a hand over his brow.

"That looks like the milk inspector. "What the hell does he want?"

"I'm sure it's nothing," Grandma said.

Sighing, an unhappy Charles slammed back out the door and headed for the barn, stomach growling all the way.

Ruthy and Callie were still in the barn. The 3,000 square foot, rectangular, concrete floor where the cows were herded to wait for their turn to be milked was littered with manure from this morning. Ruthy pushed a long-handled scraper over the main floor, shoving the manure into two-foot wide gutters on either side. At a foot and a half deep, the gutters were filling up quickly. From those, the manure would go down a conveyance and out of the barn and into a waiting manure spreader.

Callie, armed with a pitchfork, was emptying straw bedding out of the nearby calf-enclosure. The girls were silent, focused on the tasks at hand, though the radio played softly in the background.

Will I see you...in September? The voice on the radio crooned. *Or lose you to a summer love...*

The cattle, in the field just outside the barn door, bellered despondently as if they were empathizing with the song. The sound was maddening. Had there been only one or two, it may have been tolerable, but there were over a hundred of them, voices combined in a desolate chorus.

"I wonder if Adam will be home by September," Ruthy said. "I miss him so much."

"I know, Ruthy, but he'll be back. You'll see."

Charles had made the milk-house by that time and was speaking with the inspector.

298

"I need a minute of your time, Mr. Barnes. There's something we need to discuss."

Ruthy sighed. "I don't know. I wouldn't blame him if he left and never came back."

"No kidding, me either. Man! When Bull went after him--geez! I've never been so scared in my whole life!" Callie stopped and rested her tired arm on the pitchfork. "But he loves you, Ruthy, and I don't think he's going to let some stupid bull stop him. He didn't let Daddy stop him, did he?"

"No. He didn't, did he?" Ruthy looked down at her watch. "Uh oh, it's time for lunch. We'd better get a move on before Daddy comes out here looking for us."

Callie turned and made to renew her effort. Just as she began to jab the fork into the pile of bedding, a gray, blur of movement caught her attention out of the corner of her eye. A rat! And it was running her way!

Her aim went wild and instead of hitting the pile of straw, she drove the pitchfork straight into the top of her right foot. The rat halted and did a turn-about as she fell to the floor, moaning in agony. Ruthy rushed over. She couldn't see much through the green rubber boots that Callie was wearing, but she could see that at least two of the tines were buried in her sister's foot. Vomit made its way up from her stomach and into her throat and she fought desperately not to throw up.

"Oh my God! She screamed. "Hang on! I'll go and get some help." Ruthy ran for the milk-house.

As she ran through the milk-house door, she saw the inspector talking with her father, but it didn't register with her as being important.

"Daddy!" She blurted. "Daddy, I need help!"

"Not right now, Ruth-Ann," he hissed. Can't you see I'm talking?"

"The milk tested positive for some kind of bacterial infection," the milk inspector said.

"What the hell do you mean bacterial infection?" Charles fumed, ignoring Ruthy's nervous pacing. "You Sons-a-Bitches! There ain't a goddamned thing wrong with my cows. You're just trying to get out of payin' me what I got comin'."

Charles did not mention the fact that he'd already found six cows dead in the field this week. And not just dead, but torn, literally, to pieces. He was almost certain that they'd been trampled by the rest of the herd.

"Listen, Mr. Barnes, there *is* something wrong with these cows. Listen to them! Jesus, I don't know how you can stand it! I've only been here five minutes and it's already driving me crazy. Healthy cows don't do that. Healthy cows don't sound like that."

"DADDY!—"

"Not now, I said," Charles' face was red, eyes narrowed.

"But, Daddy, I need help!"

"NOT RIGHT NOW, GIRL! ARE YOU FUCKING DEAF?"

Helplessly, Ruthy turned and darted back out the milk-house door.

"Look," the inspector said earnestly. "All I know's that the milk tested positive for *something*. We had to dump the whole load."

"The whole fucking load?"

"We couldn't identify the bacteria. We've never seen anything like it before and we don't know what it means. You're going to have to get a vet in here and have this entire herd checked out."

"Really? And just how in the hell do you figure I'm going to pay for all that, since you threw away the milk that was going to make my check this month? I'm guessing you ain't gonna foot the bill."

"I'm sorry, Mr. Barnes. There's nothing I can do. We can't accept any more tanks from this farm without a clean bill of health."

"I guess I could call the slaughterhouse..." Charles thought out loud. "Maybe make enough money off of the meat to buy some new ones."

"What? You've got to be kidding me!" The inspector was getting angry now. "You can't sell the meat until you find out what this is and deal with it. Have you got any idea what the implications of this could be?"

"Well, I ain't gonna just sit around here and let you bastards send me to the poor-house either. Christ!"

"Look. I'm not kidding around with you. You have one day to get a vet in here and find out what's going on with this herd. Tomorrow morning, bright and early, I'm calling the County Health Department, and someone will be out here looking for answers."

"Yeah?" Charles shot back. "Well for now you can get your goddamned, thieving ass off'n my property."

"More than happy to, Mr. Barnes. You have the rest of today."

And he headed for the door.

"SON-OF-A-BITCH!" Charles hollered after him as he went out. "IF YOU EVER POKE YOUR NOSE IN AROUND HERE AGAIN, I'LL KICK YOUR SORRY ASS!"

Charles drew in a deep breath and let it out slowly. He watched as the inspector got back in his car and drove out the driveway. The cows continued to bray. Charles flattened his hands over his ears.

"SHUT UP, YOU BASTARDS," he screamed. "SHUT THE HELL UP ALL READY!"

Rubbing his throbbing head, he looked around.

"Fuck it," he said. "This whole goddamned place is going to hell in a hand-car and me with it if I don't do something."

He turned and slammed through the milk-house door. The adjoining room held the big bulk-tank where the milk was stored. It was made of stainless steel and sat in a concrete pit sunk into the ground. Charles jumped into the pit and squatted down. Frustrated tears began to flow as he opened the valve near the bottom of the tank. The moments in time when Charles was on the right side of sanity mixed in with the milky-white liquid and swirled down the drain.

"Owwwwwwwww...it hurts," Callie sobbed.

"It's okay, Kiddo, I'm going to get it out."

Grimacing, Ruthy grabbed the handle of the pitchfork and pulled hesitantly. The fork stuck.

"Owwwwwwwwwwww! Ruthy, don't," Callie begged. She was holding her foot in both hands, sitting stone still.

"Hold on, Callie. I'm going to have to pull harder."

"No! Ruthy, no! It huurrrts."

"I know that but it's got to be done. There's only one way out—"

Ruthy pulled again, slightly harder this time. Callie's boot rose off the ground a few inches, but the fork remained embedded. Again the vomit rose in Ruthy's throat.

"Leave it alone," sobbed Callie. "Don't pull it again, pleeeeaaase. Isn't Daddy coming?"

"He's busy with the inspector. He won't come. You're just going to have to bear with me. There's only one way out."

Callie squeezed her eyes shut tightly. "Do it," she said, "but do it quick-like."

Ruthy's fists tightened on the handle of the pitchfork. She closed her eyes as well, as she braced herself for what was to come. She placed one foot directly behind Callie's boot and the other she lay gently over the toe in order to keep her foot stationary. Taking one deep breath, she yanked with all of her might. As the fork gave up its purchase, Callie's body slumped and her head hit the concrete hard.

"Oh, Jesus!" Ruthy grew frantic. "C'mon, Callie, not now."

She cradled Callie's head and slapped lightly on her cheeks. "Callie. I need you to wake up Callie. You're bleeding. C'mon, stay with me, Kiddo. We have to take care of this quick."

There was blood on the tines of the pitchfork. There was blood on Callie's boot...a lot of blood.

"Come on, we have to stop the bleeding," Ruthy said, seconds later when Callie had regained consciousness. "Stop the bleeding, and then soak this. That's what Mom would do. And then I'll bandage it for you. How's your head?"

"It hurts like crazy," Callie answered, gently touching the knot on her skull.

"C'mon, let's get you some ice for that while we're at it."

She helped Callie up and placed her arm over her shoulder. Supporting her in this manner, she helped her hobble to the house. Grandma and the girls were nowhere to be seen, though there was now a huge plate of roast beef sandwiches on the table. Dragging Callie into the bathroom, she partially filled the tub with warm water and Epsom salts.

Callie sat on the toilet and slowly pulled off her boot. Her previously white sock had gone over to red. There were two, perfectly round holes in the top of her foot near her toes, bits of cotton fiber from her socks stuck in the dark blood that was beginning to clot there. As she peeled her sock down over her ankle and under her heel, she began to wobble again. Jumping up, Ruthy grabbed her shoulders to steady her.

"Not again, Callie," she pleaded. "C'mon, stay with me here."

And Callie did manage to stay with her this time, but it took twenty minutes of holding towels on the wound and applying pressure before they could stop the bleeding and get her foot in the tub.

"You stay here. I'll be back in a little while to bandage this. I gotta go finish the barn floor first." And leaving Callie there to soak, she hurried back to the barn to finish the chores alone.

***

"And that's where I found her when I came into the barn," Eddie said. "I could tell right away that something was wrong just by the look on her face and the way she was scraping the floor. She was beet-red, sweating like a dog, and pushing that scraper like tomorrow wasn't coming.

"It didn't take me long to get the story out of her. The kid just needed a little help. I figured I'd run up and check on Callie first and then come back and help Ruthy. And that's what I did. I got her out of the tub, made sure nothing was broken, got some ice for her head and saw that she was settled in her bed and resting comfortably.

"At the time, I thought Callie was the one with the problem, but that was before I got back and saw what had happened to Ruthy while I was gone. And I swear, I ain't ever seen nothin' like what happened next. Not before, nor at any time after, and I hope I never do again."

CHAPTER NINETEEN

Moments later, and Ruthy still working at a feverish pace, Charles burst through the barn door. He assessed the situation in an instant.

"Ruth Ann! Where you at, Girl?" His face was a study in rage, eyes bulging out of crimson cheeks.

"Right here, Daddy." She was about three-quarters of the way down the floor.

"Do you mean to tell me that you ain't finished with this yet? What in the hell have you been doing all morning?" As he talked, he advanced.

"I'm sorry, Daddy—"

"Sorry? Sorry? Well, sorry don't get the chores done, now does it?" Half way there...

Charles posture was frightening. His shoulders were thrown back and his fists clenched tightly.

"But Callie—"

"But Callie, hell! Callie ain't got shit to do with it! Where the hell is she anyways? She's supposed to be cleaning the calf pen. I see the pile, but I don't see Callie." Ten more steps...

"She's up at the house. She's soaking—"

"I don't wanna hear no goddamned excuses! This farm don't run on excuses." Ruthy had stopped scraping. Her father stood directly in front of her now, teeth clenched, chest heaving.

"But, Daddy—"

"Don't you 'but, Daddy' me, by the Jesus! There is no goddamned reason in the world for this work not to be done. You all know what you're supposed to be doing and when you're supposed to be doing it. Now get your lazy ass moving and get this goddamned floor cleaned up. And it had better be spic and span. Now move!"

Ruthy's eyes narrowed. *Lazy? Lazy?* Fear began to eek out of her as anger flooded in. Ruthy Barnes had finally had enough. Standing up straight, she looked her father in the eye, perhaps for the first time.

"Yes, *Sir*..." she spat, but made no move to continue. "I'll get right on that for you, *Sir*."

Charles immediately raised his right arm as if to strike.

"Don't you get smart with me, you little Bitch. Not if you know what's good for you. Now, MOVE!"

Ruthy picked the scraper up in both hands and heaved it back up the barn floor.

"Clean it yourself."

"What? What the hell did you just say to me?"

Charles was close enough now that spittle sprayed in Ruthy's face. She wiped the hateful stuff away with the back of her arm. His eyes bulged with anger but she continued to stare him down.

"I said, clean it yourself, you Son-of-a-Bitch!" and she turned to walk away.

Charles leaped. He grabbed a handful of hair from the back of her head, knocking her feet out from under her, and began dragging her up the barn floor. In seconds, they'd reached the place where the scraper lay and he shoved her down beside it.

"By the Jesus, you *will* scrape this floor and every goddamned inch of it, and if you *ever* speak to me that way again, I'll kill you!"

Ruthy stood up and faced her father once again.

"MOVE!" he screamed, pointing at the scraper. "DOUBLE-TIME!"

Ruthy, having gone this far, was not turning back now.

"YOU CAN GO STRAIGHT TO HELL, FOR ALL I CARE," she shot back. "I AIN'T DOIN' IT!"

Charles fist slammed into the side of her face, knocking her straight to the floor. Once again he leaped on her and began dragging her. This time he made for the gutter and as he got there he shoved her face, full on, into the shit filled gutter.

"How's that taste, goddamn you? How's that taste in your goddamned smart mouth?"

Ruthy struggled violently as he pushed her head down further into the muck. She was in it up to her neck when he pulled her back out. Runny, green cow manure slid in globs down her neck and back as she choked and sputtered.

"I'm gonna learn you one way or another," Charles shouted, and shoved her head back into the gutter. "Wanna talk shit to me—"

"And that's what I saw when I walked back in." Eddie looked truly distressed now. "Ruthy was flailing like crazy and he was still holding her down. She was drowning in cow shit!

"'What the hell—?' I screamed and grabbed Charles beneath the arms. It took everything I had just to haul him off of her, but I did it. 'What the hell are you trying to do, kill her?' I asked.

"Ruthy rolled over and began scooping the shit out of her eyes and mouth, coughing and sputtering as she went. Charles, who was flat on his backside now, jumped to his feet.

"'Mind your business, Eddie, this doesn't concern you,' he told me.

"Charles rounded on me and squared off. I could see he meant to hit me next.

"I wasn't backing off this time either. 'Maybe not,' I said, 'but I'm not gonna stand by and watch you kill this kid. You'll have to get through me first.'

"Ruthy ran for the house.

"And then he did hit me. He threw a punch and I threw a punch, and we wrestled around a bit, calling one another every name we could. And then it was over...almost. As we stood up and began brushing ourselves off, he said just two words to me. Just two words. But those two words were enough to prove to me what an idiot I was.

"Charles looked at me, the blood dripping off of his split lip, and said, 'You're fired."

"Good Lord," Father Murphy said, drawing a breath. "Good Lord."

"All I could say was, 'What?' It hit home all at once what a fool I'd been.

"And Charles said, 'Get the hell off'n my property now.'

"And that was it. Charles Barnes never lost.

"I spent the next couple of hours driving around. I wasn't going anywhere, just riding the roads. I was a man without a country now. No job, no home, and worse—I couldn't do anything to help the kids anymore. Charles Barnes was mad as a hatter.

"I was beside myself with worry and a hundred different plans ran through my mind. I could go to Annette's job and tell her what happened. That wouldn't work because she'd just rush home and the fight would break out again. It was liable to be worse this time. I had no doubt that someone was going to get hurt. I could go back, apologize...but again, that would only make things worse. And I'd probably end up in jail.

"I finally settled on the Sheriff. Sure as hell he could stop Charles. He had a badge and a gun. I stormed into his office at about four o'clock and poured out the whole story. He looked highly skeptical as he filled out the report. By then, I was so worried that I probably did sound half-crazed. Still, I finished the story and he promised to go down there and check it out.

"What I didn't know until later, is that the minute I left there he tossed the paperwork into the trash.

"I can see him now, saying, 'A man's children are his own business, and I'll have none of it."

CHAPTER TWENTY

When Charles next entered the dining room he carried a .45 caliber pistol in one hand and a padlock in the other. The key was in his pocket.

"Ma, take the two little girls up to your apartment for a bit."

Grandma was more than a little taken back by the request, but the look on Charles' face told her he meant business. Dropping her crocheting on the end table she ushered Jenny and Dawny out of the room.

"Hank, you round up Mark and the other three girls and take them to the barn. You'll be doin' the milkin' without me tonight. Not that the milk matters, but maybe it'll shut those cows the hell up for a while."

Hank, who'd only come in from the field for a quick drink, knew nothing of the day's events.

"Okay," he said tentatively, eyeing the gun. "Is something wrong, Charles?"

"Nothing I can't handle. You go on now."

Hank set the glass down and left immediately. Charles sat down at the dining room table to wait. As he sat, he stared straight ahead at the bathroom door. He could hear the water splashing in the bathtub. He lay the gun down in his lap and the padlock on the table. Leaning back he began to whistle softly. While the minutes passed, the whistle turned into words and he drummed on the table with his fingers as he sang.

I hear that train a comin'
Rolling round the bend

And I ain't seen the sunshine since...
I don't know when...

Tap, tap, hum...

When I was just a baby, my mama told me, Son,
Always be a good boy, don't ever play with guns.

Tap, tap...

But I shot a man in Reno...just to watch him die...

Tap, tap, hum...

Now I'm stuck in Folsom prison, and time keeps draggin' on—

Just then the bathroom door opened and Ruthy stepped out wearing a faded, blue robe and wet hair. She didn't see Charles at first, and started towards the hallway.

"Whoa, there! Where ya goin' in such a hurry, girl?"

Ruthy froze.

"Sit down," Charles ordered.

Ruthy drew a breath and made her way gingerly to the table. She seated herself across from Charles and waited.

"That was some show you put on down there in the barn today."

He was calm. Too calm.

"I'm sorry, Daddy. I don't know what got into me."

Her eye was blackening up nicely.

"No? Well, I do. It's all your mother's doing, that's what. I tried to tell her, but she wouldn't listen."

"Don't blame Mom. It's not her fault. I did it and I'll take the punishment for it."

"Oh, you'll take your punishment, all right. You'll do that." Charles eyes grew calculating as he studied her face. "But you won't do it under my roof no more."

"Huh?" Ruthy asked. "What do you mean?"

"I mean, I ain't havin' no smart mouthed, worthless, lazy Sons-a-Bitches livin' on my farm. That's what I mean."

Ruthy's face wore a look of incredulity.

"Are you telling me to leave, Daddy? You're kicking me out?"

"Nope. You ain't goin' nowhere tonight. But I did make a little phone call while you were in getting all prettied up. I called the lady from Social Services."

"Social Services?"

"Yup! Told her that I had me one of them worthless, incorrigible children living with me. Told her that you don't want to listen and do what you're told. Told her that you had a dirty mouth, callin' your own father filthy names and refusin' to help with the chores. Told her you were a thief too."

Ruthy now wore a look of sheer horror on her face.

"I'll help, Daddy. I will. I'm sorry—"

"Nope. Too late now. She'll be here tomorrow and she's takin' you with her. You're going to go and live in a state home where kids like you belong."

"Daddy, no!" Ruthy pleaded. "I'm sorry. I'll never give you a hard time again. Please?" She was crying now, and obviously frightened.

"What's done is done," he sneered. "Now you go on up and pack your clothes."

Ruthy, desperate for anything other, begged, "No, Daddy, don't make me go. I don't want to go."

"Well, you should have thought about that earlier, Missy! You should have thought about that before you went and gave me such a hard time. Cost me my best hired man too. Well I'm washing my hands of you."

Too frightened and confused to think about what she was saying, Ruthy panicked, "I'll run away, then. I'll run away, Daddy, before I go off with some Social Services lady."

"Yeah, I thought you might say that," Charles responded, bringing the pistol up from his lap and leveling it at her face. "But I don't think you really want to try it."

"Wha--?" Ruthy gasped. Her face crumpled. "Daddy?" Her voice was high and uncertain now, like a badly frightened child.

"You're a ward of the state now and you ain't gonna be running away on my watch," he answered. Picking the padlock up in his other hand, he commanded, "Let's go now. I'm gonna have to lock you up!"

He rose to his feet and motioned for her to do the same. Ruthy looked around for help from anywhere. There was none. She dare not speak, but rose as he'd asked. He used the gun to motion her toward the hallway. She walked stiffly in front of him, towards the stairwell.

Up, he motioned. She climbed. When they reached the second floor she turned right and followed the banister up the landing towards her bedroom. Mistakenly thinking that he was going to lock her in her bedroom, she started to turn left at the end of the landing.

"Not there," he said firmly. "There!" And with the pistol, he pointed to the attic steps.

Ruthy looked around in horror. "Daddy, no!" she begged. "Please don't make me go back up there." A fresh crop of tears flowed down her cheeks.

Charles grabbed her once again by the hair on the back of her head. He brought the pistol up and pressed it tightly into her skull.

"You're singin' a different tune now, ain't ya?" he hissed. "Christ! You sound just like those goddamned bellering cows out there. Now move."

And within seconds, Ruthy was up the attic stairs and the padlock was thrown through the hasp to the attic door.

"And I'd better not hear one goddamned sound out of you," Charles yelled through the trap-door. "Because if I have to come up there..."

He sat down on the steps below. He'd stand guard all night if need be, but tomorrow that child would be leaving with the woman from the state.

Trapped in the attic, Ruthy's mind was reeling with shock. Knowing that her father waited below, she dare not make a sound. She ran an emotional gamut between rage, and pain, and confusion. *How could he?* And then fear set in again.

She ran for the cupola, where the last remnants of afternoon sunlight washed in through the windows. They were too narrow to afford an escape and she was too frightened to try the windows below. There was nothing for it but to sit and wait. Her mother would be home soon.

Ruthy forgot that Annette was working overtime.

CHAPTER TWENTY-ONE

Tears leaked out of Ongwaterohiathe's eyes as he spoke. He lay on a pallet near the council fire, which was circled all around by natives. Hadawa'ko and Emma sat cross-legged on the ground next to him.

The wound was insidious. And it was deep. Throughout the long night, the False Face Society had labored over him, chasing the evil spirits and bad medicine into the darkness. The poison that lingered was one of a spiritual nature rather than physical. Its recipe was sadness and despair and it contained the imprint of a hundred killing wars, a thousand tragedies, a million sons and daughters lost...of hunger, and of violence, and of unspeakable pain. It was oppressive and it took the strength of Atlas for the Light-Keeper to raise his head now.

He had just finished the retelling of Jenny's dream.

"Winter has come to the heart of the Haudenosaunee nation," he said. "Our sons and daughters are herded onto reservations like cattle. They struggle with addiction and poverty. Poverty! There was no poverty when our people were free. The white man created poverty when he began to count wealth instead of giving thanks for it."

At this, he lowered his head and wept openly. Around the edges of the clearing an assortment of souls shuffled nervously about. They had come here looking for the portal. Without the guidance of the Light-Keeper they were lost. Another, darker figure stood just inside the tree line, just out of sight of the council. He waited and listened.

"Long ago," he went on, "the Peacemaker, Deganawada instructed our people to bury the weapons of war under the sacred roots of the Tree of Peace. Never again should brother kill brother. The five nations were united. The Oneida, the Mohawk, the Seneca, the Cayuga, and the Onondaga were joined under the Great Tree. Later, the Tuscarora came from the south and entered into the union."

Ongwaterohiathe stopped momentarily to regain his faltering strength. Hadawa'ko grasped the pendant which hung around his neck. His fingers caressed the lines of the Tree of Peace which had been carved on it.

The Light-Keeper continued.

"For many moons we lived by this law. But now our people have uncovered the weapons from the sacred root. They fight among themselves again, but they do not fight over grave injustices. They fight over white man's trinkets! The Great Law of Peace is broken."

Heads nodded in agreement from around the fire.

"Orenda sends the broken rainbow to us in a dream," Ongwaterohiathe continued. "It is a sign. This child carries the spirit of Deganawada within her. She has the power to make the rainbow whole again. She can mend the peace and heal the anger; brother against brother, red man against white."

Again, heads nodded and there were murmurs of agreement from all around.

"But her path is forked," he went on. "And great danger lies ahead. There is an evil that lives inside her dreams, inside that house."

"I have seen this spirit!" Hadawa'ko exclaimed.

Just then the dark figure stepped out from behind the trees. "I also know this spirit," he said.

"Papa!" Emma shrieked. She leapt to her feet and ran to her father, nearly knocking him over with her enthusiastic hug. "I am so happy you came."

She took the dowser by the hand and led him back to the fire. Hadawa'ko rose and shook his hand and he seated himself to the side of Ongwaterohiathe's pallet, next to the chief.

"It is an honor to join the council again," Justus said. The natives acknowledged this fact with smiles and nods. Emma seated herself next to her father, and once again took his hand.

"I am sorry I'm late," Justus said. "Please go on."

Chief Hadawa'ko took up the story here.

"The one you speak of is old and should have come here long ago. He fears the great beyond and will not come. There are others there too but he keeps them from the portal."

"And he's strong," Justus added. "He feeds off of Charles Barnes' anger. I have been watching for some time. He grows stronger by the minute. The children are living in fear."

"He is dark," Ongwaterohiathe said, "and has bad medicine. He plays a game with them, but in the end, he will take them all. He will take them and bind them to him and keep them in that house forever!"

"Surely, Sir, you cannot suggest that we allow this to happen? Is there nothing we can do to stop him?" Justus asked.

Hadawa'ko nodded his head in agreement.

"I would fight," he said.

"It is not for us to interfere," Ongwaterohiathe repeated. "The Great Spirit has a plan."

Justus rose angrily.

"The Great Spirit!" he sneered. "God, the almighty...it doesn't matter what you call him, we all worship the same being. And while we're sitting here waiting for the Great Spirit's plan to unfold they're being beaten by their own father. While we sit and talk, the evil in that attic grows. They're just children! They should be out playing in the sunshine."

"There is no hope," Ongwaterohiathe answered. "I was there. I walked the dream."

"There's always hope," Justus said. "I had hoped to bring this to an end with the water. We use the tools that we are given. In the beginning I just wanted them to go away. I thought to drive them out before Charles' energy made that spirit strong again. I hoped they could make a fresh start elsewhere, and the evil would quiet down." He sighed. "But I failed."

"You *interfered*," Ongwaterohiathe said firmly.

"Yes, I interfered," Justus admitted. "And it's come to naught. But someone's got to fight the fights. Someone has to do *something*! Don't you see that?"

Ongwaterohiathe looked dubious.

"For the love of God, Man, and all that's holy! We're here for a reason. It's the love that binds us to this earth; love of this land, love of our children, love of *his* children for that matter! We're wasting time. I would not see this go on another moment while we wait around for the plan. We *are* the plan, damnit! We *are* the plan."

Ongwaterohiathe was visibly struck by this realization and the curtain of doggedness began to draw back from his eyes. Little by little, a new, determination overtook him.

"I see the truth in your words," he said. "Let us speak no more. Summon the horses. We ride!"

CHAPTER TWENTY-TWO

In the cupola, Ruthy lay sleeping long after the last rays of sunshine had retreated, making way for nightfall. She had cried herself into a state of exhaustion waiting for Annette to return and set things to right. Charles remained at his post on the stairs below and the other Barnes children had been sent to their rooms for the evening.

Randall, who'd been skulking about for some time now, was practicing tip-toeing across the creaky, old floor. Back and forth he went, comically lifting one foot at a time off the floor, pointing his toes and then placing his foot down as gently as possible so as not to make a sound.

"Shhhh," he whispered softly at Ruthy, laying pointer finger to pursed lips, "don't want to wake up the kid."

His face took on the look of one giggling, though he held back any sound. When he was certain that he had mastered the technique, he wandered over to where the girl slept. Bending down, he reached his long, spindly arms underneath her, and ever so gently picked her up. This, he did, with all the sensitivity of a mother carrying her sleeping child into bed at night. Ruthy stirred momentarily, shifting her weight and placing her arms tightly around his neck.

Randall looked very pleased as he carried Ruthy down the steps toward his room below, tip-toeing all the way.

A short while later, having grown chilled, Ruthy awoke to find herself chained to the wall in his room with the others. Immediately frozen in terror, she was unable to make a sound.

"Roothy Do! You're awake!" he chortled. "Good to see you back, Girl, though I hate to say I told you so!"

Randall's comrades were looking at her as though they had just swallowed something unpleasant. Randall had shifted them all around, taking full advantage of each of the four walls of the square room. On Ruthy's right side, fifteen to twenty men and women were terribly crowded in upon one another. She recognized some of the faces, though today they were all dressed in their Sunday best. It was as though they had bathed and dressed for some special occasion; black suits, bowties and hats for the gentlemen, and proper dresses and bonnets for the ladies.

Ruthy, separate from any other, was chained to the middle of the back wall.

On the other wall, the one to her left, were two solitary souls. One being the little girl who'd taken to her the first time she was here. The other, a young man with sensitive eyes and unruly hair, obviously suffered from Down's syndrome. It was difficult to say what color that hair might be as all of these people presented eerily in black and white and shades of gray.

Toward the front of the room, on the remaining wall, stood Randall. He was also dressed in traditional garb, though the black clothing only served to make him look even more thin, pant legs and shirt sleeves much too short for his long, gaunt frame. He had a hammer in one hand and was just finishing up with his latest building project. He had created an old-fashioned gallows, much like the ones Ruthy had seen portrayed on TV in black and white, spaghetti westerns. A chalk-board had been mounted to the wall beside the gallows.

"Is she going to stay this time?" asked the child. "Is she going to be my Mommy now?"

Constance Godwin, Ruthy thought. *1896-1908. Death by starvation...* And then, *where'd that come from?*

"Well, now, I think that's gonna be a great, big YES, Constance!" Randall answered giggling. "Ruthy's come home to play and I think she's here to stay."

"Lemme go," Ruthy pleaded meekly. She was badly frightened and the tinny quality of her voice confirmed that fact. "You can't keep me here."

"Oh, but I can," Randall answered. "Try and get out."

She began to struggle with the shackles on her wrists, causing them to bite more deeply. It was cold in the room and the bad smell was back. No amount of lye soap could clean the air in here.

"No use wearing yourself out, Missy," said the dead, old man closest to her, on the right. "You ain't goin' nowheres."

With hair that had gone entirely over to white, he had finely sculpted cheekbones, hard eyes and lips that were set in a grim, straight line. A week's worth of stubble covered his pale chin. He wore what looked to Ruthy like a well-worn, civil war uniform. The name Eamon popped into Ruthy's head, as if she were merely recognizing an old acquaintance.

Eamon, she thought...*Eamon McGee, 1808-1870, taken with Alcoholism, died of Marasmus, a progressive emaciation due to an enfeebled constitution...*

Visions from his life began to wander aimlessly before her eyes; Eamon McGee, hungry and weary, deep in the heart of some God-forsaken, Southern swamp during the war, Eamon McGee coming home to find his wife and sons all dead from the Small Pox, Eamon McGee chained up in this very attic, shivering violently from the cold, the stench of urine and feces rising up around him.

343

In his hands he held a battered, tin plate, cold, watery, gray gruel spreading across it and onto a single crust of moldy bread. He was eating it with his fingers. As he held the plate out for Ruthy to see, the head of a solitary worm wriggled out of its lumpy center. Eamon McGee plunged his fingers into the gruel, pulled out the small, brown form and smeared it on his greasy pants leg. His dark eyes were a study in hopelessness as he plunged his fingers back in for another bite.

"Nope, won't get ya nowhere at all," sneered the woman on her left. "Ruthy doooooo."

It was as if she was jealous. The name Agnes occurred to Ruthy. Agnes looked just plain mean-spirited. Small in stature, she was thin and wiry. Her face took on an almost masculine form, with a hookish nose and stern slits for eyes. Her hair was pinned back in a tight bun. She was dressed in a prim, black

344

and gray pin-striped dress with white lace around the neck.

Agnes, Ruthy thought. *Agnes Huddersfield, 1874-1910, suffered from nervous prostration and bouts of hysteria, dejected, she took her own life...*

Ruthy saw through the eyes of Agnes Huddersfield momentarily, saw the other children in the schoolyard mocking her, heard the insults they threw cruelly at the homely, young girl. She saw a handsome young man taking the hand of a far prettier girl in marriage. And more than that, Ruthy felt a great desolation from within, a cold, emptiness of spirit that flowed like a river through endless days and nights of drudgery. Finally, she saw Agnes lying prostrate in this attic, staring blankly at a gaping hole in the wall into which powdery, snow had entered to pile up on the floor across from her.

Ruthy struggled harder at the chains.

"Ruthy!" Randall sniggered. "Sit still, Girl! For Heaven's sake, you act like someone's gonna kill you!" His shoulders shook with laughter.

Ruthy realized that the harder she struggled, the more the chains bit into her wrists, but at least her vision cleared. She grew still and looked straight ahead, determined not to be a witness to any more of these ghastly histories.

"What are you going to do with me?" she asked. "Please don't make me stay up here. Just lemme go. Please..." she begged.

"Well now, that's gonna be entirely up to you, Roothy Do," Randall answered. "Are you good at games?"

"Games?" Ruthy asked, studying the gallows as if seeing it for the first time. "That's a game?"

"Yeah," Randall answered enthusiastically. "You've played hangman before, haven't you?"

His eyes sparkled with excitement as he studied her face.

"Good Lord! That's what this is for? Hangman? You want me to play hangman with you? With that?" Ruthy's eyes widened in horror.

"Of course, with that. That's what the gallows is for, isn't it? For hangin? Sheesh, what a dim-wit you are! No wonder your father's sick of you," Randall answered.

Ruthy hung her head.

A vertical line divided the chalkboard into two equal halves. The portion on the left remained blank. The portion on the right side was filled with what looked like dashes to Ruthy, but were actually lines marking spaces with which to fill in the letters of a phrase. It looked like a lot of letters to Ruthy. Randall wore a white stick of chalk behind his right ear.

"I don't want to play," Ruthy said.

"Well, make up your mind, Girly! Didn't you say you wanted to get out of here? As near as

I can figure it, this is the only way. Your father ain't comin' to get you and your mama's workin' late. You don't think I'm just goin' to let you waltz on out of here, do you?"

"You mean if I play hangman with you, then you'll let me go?"

"Not exactly," Randall answered. "If you play, and *win* then I'll let you go...for now. But if you play, and *lose*, well, then, by the time Mama rushes in to save you, you'll all ready be one of us, won't you?"

Putting both of his hands around his own neck, he pantomimed choking as though he'd been hanged.

"I just love a game when the stakes are right, don't you, Rooootthhy?"

He rubbed both palms together; face lighting up with maniacal glee.

Ruthy swallowed hard.

"But that's not fair—"

"Randall's Rooooles, Ruthy, remember?" His face grew menacing now. "It's the only way to play. Besides, who doesn't like hangman? It's a good game. You like hangman, don't you?"

"I don't think I like it very much the way you play it," Ruthy answered.

"Doesn't matter," Randall said. "Cuz I like it fine. Hangman's my fav-o-rite! This is going to be one fun evening! The only question left is: Are you ready to play?"

"Say, yes." said Constance. "We're on your side--me and Thomas. Well, kind of on your side. We want you to stay."

"Hmmmpfff," said a man on her right. "I wouldn't do it."

Samuel Bartlett, 1843-1862, Palsy, Marasmus, Exposure.

Ruthy kept her eyes forward, determined not to see.

"Yeah," a female voice agreed. "I wouldn't do it either. Not again, anyways."

Eliza Mary Lofthouse, 1869-1904, Apoplexy, Marasmus, Exposure.

"I *am* pretty good at games," Randall laughed. "So what do you say, Missy? Do we play today?"

"You haven't given me much choice," Ruthy answered. She prayed silently for her mother to make it home in time. If she could just stall long enough...

"Well, alrighty then! Make your first guess." Randall cried enthusiastically.

There was a sudden shift in Ruthy's consciousness as Randall shanghaied her perspective. With a whoosh, she felt as though all of the others receded into the background. Their muttering became faint, as though far away, though she could still make out the words. They had obviously divided themselves into cheering sections. Oddly, those on the right, who seemed to despise Ruthy and want her to leave, cheered for her to win. Those on the left, Candace and Thomas, who wanted her to stay, cheered for her to lose.

350

At the same time, the entire house shifted. For the first time ever, the sounds emanating from the attic were amplified below. Randall had taken his game show live and on the air.

"We love you, Ruthy," called Constance.

On the stairs below, Charles' head snapped up, his eyes opening wide.

What the hell? He thought. *Who's up there with her?* At first, he imagined her sisters had somehow gotten around him, and was furious. But that didn't feel like the right answer.

"Make it a hard one, Randall," said Constance's voice. "Hang her quick so she doesn't suffer."

Something deep in the pit of Charles' stomach felt wrong. His skin crawled and he began to smell the horrible stench coming from the attic. Suddenly, he knew that Ruthy's tale of something alive in the attic had been true. His mind, badly diseased from the bacteria in the water, and overwhelmed by the noise and confusion to boot, locked up. He did not know what to do. Desperation set in and he rose and began pacing up and down the stairs like a caged animal. He pulled the key from his pocket and grabbed the padlock with the intention of releasing her.

"C'mon, guess a letter, Bitch!" said one of the ghouls.

Charles froze. Panic set in and breathing became difficult. His hands shook as he gripped the handle of the pistol more tightly.

Another of Randall's inmates checked in, "Yeah, choose a letter, Ruthy. Any letter to start."

Charles tried once again to put key to lock, but was unable. The sound of the cows bellering in the barnyard mixed in with the sounds coming from the attic. Well, not exactly bellering...he had never heard sounds like this coming from cattle before. They were more like shrieks of rage. It sounded as though they were tearing one another apart out there. The sound of splintering wood added to the cacophony as they began to run head on into the barn door.

What the hell was going on? Nothing made sense anymore. He was confused and angry, but mostly, he was afraid. And he was angry *because* he was afraid.

"What am I gonna do?" he asked himself. He thought he should go up there, but God knew what he'd find. Those voices were so...dead-sounding. He thought just a moment longer, and in that moment his anger pushed the fear aside and took the lead.

"She's a thief and a liar," he pronounced.

This seemed to make the most sense to him.

"Well, to hell with her! She has to take her medicine. She shouldn't of disrespected me. She has to pay the price, by the Jesus! She's on her own now and see how she likes it."

He put the key back in his pocket and with new resolve, sat back down on the steps. He covered both of his ears with his hands. Between the game of hangman above and the war from the barnyard, the noise was deafening. Frustrated tears streamed from his eyes.

I hear that train a comin', he hummed, trying to drown out the sounds.

In the attic, front and center, Ruthy saw only the chalkboard and gallows. The dashes were arranged thusly:

—— ——— —————— —— ——— ——————

Ruthy studied them as though they held any clue. When she played with her sisters, she always chose one of the most common consonants first, but which one? She'd never played for her life before.

"M," she said.

"Oh!" cried Randall. "Wrong-o, Roothy! No M here."

He turned and drew a circle roughly resembling a head on the chalkboard.

Again, Ruthy's perception was wrenched away from her. Suddenly, she found herself looking at her own body from her head's new position in the gallows. Her head was in the noose! Her body, sans head, remained chained to the wall opposite her. She saw, rather than felt the urine puddling beneath her body on the floor.

CHAPTER TWENTY-THREE

"I tried to ignore them. I tried to tell myself that I was out of the picture. That Son-of-a-bitch had fired me, hadn't he? There was nothing I could do anymore." Eddie shifted in his chair again. The light was fading and the shadows began to grow long. Father Murphy waited for him to go on.

"That was probably about the time that old, black and white image began to flash inside my head," he said. "Off, on, off, on, the picture of the house popped into my vision like a blinking caution light. The strangers were there again. I didn't know them, but I knew who they were. Hopelessness was written all over the faces that looked at me from the windows above. Hopelessness and a good-sized dose of crazy. But the strobe effect of that image in my mind, coupled with the thought of what could be happening at the Barnes' farm right now just about drove me crazy. I couldn't get it out of my mind.

"Still an hour's drive away, I wheeled my truck around and stomped on the gas pedal. For the love of Christ, I had to do something!"

***

Callie, Beth, Bonny and Mark rushed to the bottom of the attic stairs. The sounds of the game above were loud and the children were visibly upset. The disheveled condition of their father only served to frighten them more.

Mark, who had thought to jump into his father's lap, stopped short when he saw the gun.

"What is it, Daddy? What's all that hollering? Is Ruthy all right?"

"Daddy?" Beth asked anxiously, "What's wrong, Daddy? What's all that noise?"

Charles glared.

"You kids just go on back to your rooms now. I got this situation all under control," he said firmly.

The sound of booing came from above. Ruthy had made another incorrect guess.

"No sireeeee, Bob," cackled Randall. "No N in this one! Oooohhhh, that's two wrong!"

Ruthy's body hurled itself through the air and slammed onto her head in the noose. Her arms dangled loosely from the chains, attached, at the shoulders, to nothing.

"Guess again, Rooooothy Doooo!"

The remaining two hired men ran to the foot of the attic stairs as well.

Charles didn't even give them the
opportunity to speak.

"You two take your sorry asses down to the
barn and shut those cows the hell up! All this
noise is driving me crazy."

"But—" began Hank.

"NOW!" screamed Charles. "I SAID GO
AND I MEAN RIGHT, FUCKING NOW!" He
brought the pistol up and leveled it at Hank's
head.

"Yes, sir," answered Hank. The two backed
slowly towards the second floor landing and
were gone. Moments later the sound of a car
engine told just how gone they were.

"Daddy? Are you going to shoot
someone?" asked Mark. "Are you going to
shoot them people up in the attic?"

"Son? Do you hear that noise up there?"
Charles asked.

"Yes, Daddy, But what is it? I'm scared."

"That's the sound you hear when the
goddamned devil himself comes to get bad

kids! That's the sound of your sister takin' her medicine."

Marks eyes widened in horror. All four children were speechless.

"Now, you four don't want to change places with her, do you? You don't want to end up where the bad kids go. Do you?"

No answer.

"SAY!"

"No, sir," Mark answered.

"Then I suggest you get your nosy, little asses in gear and get...BACK...TO YOUR ROOMS. DOUBLE-TIME!"

All four kids hit the stairs running.

Charles lay the gun back down in his lap, covered his ears once again, and prayed to God in Heaven to make them all shut the hell up.

***

Some twenty miles away, Annette was in her car on the way home. It had been a long day, for sure, and she was tired. She reasoned that that was the cause of the uneasy feeling she had inside. Something just wasn't right. This was the first time she had closed the store by herself and she went over the procedure in her mind, visualizing herself turning off each light and locking each of the doors.

Suddenly, she froze. *Damnit!* She realized that she'd forgotten to lock the back door of the office. This was the one vendors used. Sighing, she looked for a place to turn around. It was full on nighttime now, and she was god-awful tired, but there was nothing for it. She'd have to go back.

***

The sound carried to Grandma's apartment as well. Jenny and Dawny sat huddled together in front of their Grandmother's chair, on the living room floor.

"What is it, Grandma?" Dawny asked.

"Probably just the TV from downstairs," Grandma answered. She looked dubious. Nervous even. "Although why in Heaven's name they need to play it so loud, I'll never know. You two just mind your P's and Q's and I'll go and see what it is. Stay here," she ordered.

Her face, however, contorted in that way it did when she began to drift. Momentary confusion set in, and then at once, there was a clearing up of it.

"We have to hurry!" Grandma said. "Thank Goodness Papa let me come on ahead."

"Emma!" cried the girls, in unison.

"Papa's on his way," said a breathless Emma through Grandma Barnes' mouth, "but they have to travel slowly because Ongwaterohiathe is still weak. We cannot wait for them."

362

"Where we goin', Emma?" asked Dawny. "What's happening?"

"T is correct." boomed Randall's voice from the attic. "Well done, Ruthy, four T's. You hit the mother lode that time, I'd say."

The crowd cheered.

"Let's go," cried Emma. "Ruthy's up there...with *him!* We have to try to help her."

She hauled Grandma Barnes' hefty body up and out of the chair and grabbed the two little girls by the hand. Together, they headed for the back entrance off of the living room.

The door opened up onto an exterior stairwell, which descended from the back of the house. As they climbed down, she cautioned them to be as quiet as they could. The going was painfully slow with Grandma's rickety, old body.

Just to the left of the stairs, at the bottom, lay the doors to the cellar.

"Oh, no," Jenny said weakly. "I can't. I can't go back down there."

363

"We've got to. Ruthy's in trouble," hissed Emma. "Besides, he's not down there this time. He's up there."

She pointed toward the top of the house.

"I'm scared," Dawny cried, seeing her sister's fear. "Why do we have to go down there, Emma?"

She jerked her hand out of Emma's and planted her feet.

Emma reeled on the two little girls.

"Listen, you two, and listen good. We have got to get up in that attic and this is the only way. Ruthy needs help and I don't have time for you to be acting like babies right now. We're all she has."

She grabbed the handle of the above-ground door and heaved.

"Now are you coming to help me or do I have to do this by myself?"

Jenny and Dawny reluctantly followed her into the darkened cellar, hand in hand. There was just enough moonlight for them to pick

their way through the shadowy interior. Jenny
noticed that the cellar had become, once
again, as in her dream. It was filled with the
good scent of drying flowers and herbs, and
once again there were the strange bins and
baskets of roots.

The threesome made their way around the
spring and past Emma's stone bench. Emma
led them around the corner and to the
darkened stone room that she had brought
Jenny to on that earlier day when she'd given
her the journal.

As they entered, Emma fumbled around
until her hands found a battered tin box on the
shelf. Removing a candle stubb and some
matches, she quickly lit up the area.

"Okay, where is it?" she mumbled,
surveying the walls by candlelight. "It's been
such a long time..."

"Right," she answered herself. "I
remember."

Bending down, Emma heaved on an old crate, moving it to one side. Behind it a simple, wooden door, half the size of a normal one, was revealed. Quickly, she threw the hasp, revealing a dusty stairwell. It was very narrow, only wide enough to go single file, and ascended at a very steep angle.

"Papa built this when there began to be tension between the Indians and the settlers. He feared there may be trouble. This way!" she cried and crawled in.

Jenny and Dawny followed and the three made their way quickly up towards the attic.

***

Annette arrived back at the store only to find that the back door was, indeed, locked. By this time, the uneasy feeling had built to one of near panic. She had no idea what was wrong, but knew that something was horribly, horribly out of kilter. She raced for her car again and for home.

***

"I raced as well," Eddie sighed. "I only wish now that I had turned around ten minutes earlier."

CHAPTER TWENTY-FOUR

The puzzle now looked like this:

I_ I_ _ _ _ _ I_R _ _

I_ _ S_ _ _ LS

Ruthy had guessed all of the common consonants she could think of. Her legs, only, remained in their spot by the wall, her head, neck and arms already in the noose. It was getting harder to breathe each time she guessed incorrectly as the noose tightened under the burgeoning weight of each added portion of her body. She had absolutely no idea what the answer to this puzzle could be. She was mulling over the possible vowels the puzzle might contain.

Growing restless, the crowd began to taunt her.

"Are ye a half-wit?" came a deep voice from the corner.

Emanuel Tattersall, 1795-1843, Preacher, Infirmity of Age...

Ruthy refused to look at him and instead looked straight ahead. She focused on her own legs, focused on keeping them in their place at the opposite end of the room.

Randall stood staring at her, hands on his hips and tapping one foot.

Randall Abraham Pratt, 1820-1841, Hanged by the neck until dead...

Agnes shot out from her place on the wall, to the end of her chains and spat at Ruthy. The spittle flew in her direction and hit the floor

where her feet would soon hang if she got this
one wrong.

"Idiot!" she cried. "Dolt!"

"O," Ruthy yelled. "I guess an O."

"Well done!" screeched Randall. "You *are*
good at this."

He turned to the chalkboard and began
sketching in the letters. The puzzle now
looked like this:

$$\underline{I}\,\underline{O}\quad\underline{I}\,\_\,\_\quad\_\,\_\,\_\,\underline{I}\,\underline{O}\,\underline{R}\quad\_\,\underline{O}$$

$$\underline{I}\,\_\,\_\quad\underline{S}\,\_\,\underline{O}\,\_\,\underline{L}\,\underline{S}$$

A,E,I,O and U, Ruthy ran the list of vowels
through her head.

"I," she said, "No,wait! E."

"Well, which is it, little lady?" asked Randall.
"I, or E?"

"I," she shouted.

"Ding, ding, ding! The Lady gets another
letter."

He filled in the I's and stepped aside so that
Ruthy could see the puzzle.

T̲o̲ T̲__ _I̲_T̲o̲R̲ _o̲
T̲__ S̲_o̲I̲L̲S̲

Ruthy quickly realized that the second and forth words had to be the word 'the'. And then she knew.

"To the victor go the spoils!" she shouted. "I got it didn't I? That's it, right?"

"Abso-tively, poso-lutely right, Rooooothhhy Dooooooo!" Randall hollered. "Co-rrect!"

Ruthy gasped as her body left the gallows and slammed back into the wall. Relief washed over her and she gulped at the air which entered her lungs freely again. Immediately she began to gag on the putrid stuff. The crowd commenced cheering.

"To the victor, go the spoils," Randall repeated happily. "Like now, Ruthy. Like this game."

Ruthy's stomach knotted as she realized the puzzle had been a message to her from Randall. The chains were biting into her wrists

371

again and she wasn't much more comfortable here than hanging on the gallows.

"Your turn now," she suggested, hoping that he might undo her shackles and allow her to at least stand at the chalkboard.

"Awwwww, Ruthy, you just don't understand do you? What would be the point? I've been hanged once already and I got but one neck to give to my country. Shouldn't of borrowed those horses," he chuckled.

With that, he tipped his head back revealing an ugly, red welt around his neck.

"Your turn again, Ruthy."

"But that's not fair," she protested.

"Ummm...Randall's Rules? How many times do you have to be told, Girly?"

Randall met Agnes' gaze.

"She really is a dolt, isn't she?" he asked.

Agnes chuckled.

"Anyone have a good one for the next puzzle?" he asked the crowd.

Several hands raised, and Randall began polling the crowd, stopping by each raised hand and lowering his head so the suggestion could be whispered in his ear. When he heard Agnes' suggestion his face lit up.

"Another winner!" he screeched with delight. "Ding, ding, ding!"
He skipped back to the chalkboard and began drawing the dashes for the new phrase.

"Done." he pronounced, and Ruthy saw this:

_ _ _   _ _ _ _ _ _   _ _ _ _

_ _ _ _

She decided to start with a vowel this time.
"A," she said.
"BRAVO!" Randall shouted. "Starting out on the right foot this time."
He thought about this statement for a moment and then laughed.

"No. That would make you hanging upside down, wouldn't it? Funny, but not very effective, I'd say."

The puzzle looked like this:

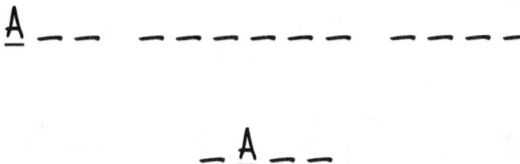

"I," said Ruthy, eyes straight ahead, though now she was looking straight at the noose in an effort to avoid Randall's gaze. She didn't want to know one more thing about his life.

"Right-O," said Randall.

Several guesses later and the puzzle looked like this:

A L L _ _ I _ _ S _ _ S I

P A S S

Although her head was in the noose again, Ruthy was pretty sure she knew the answer to this one already.

"T," she said confidently.

The crowd cheered as Randall filled in the T.

```
ALL  I_I__S  __SI

     PASS
```

"All things must pass!" Ruthy shouted. Elation soon turned to horror though and she went white as a sheet as the message slammed home.

"Are we done yet? Can I go now?" she asked meekly. "I guessed the phrase."

"Ho, ho," Randall laughed. "Three times pays for all. I got one more for ya, Roothy and this one's a doozy."

When Randall had done with the chalkboard this time it looked like this:

__   ____   ___   ___

_ _ _ _ _

Ruthy's confidence had more than wavered; it had packed its things and taken the fast train out of town. She was certain that her luck wouldn't hold for one more round. Where was her mother? Where were her sisters and her father? Would no one help her then? She resigned herself to the feel of the noose on her neck one more time.

"S," she said.

Nine guesses later, and deeply in trouble, the puzzle looked like this:

__   _E S_   F__   __E

_I_E_

Ruthy hadn't one clue. She was in it up to her head, neck, both arms and one leg. She gulped wildly for each breath of air. So many letters to go and just one more wrong guess and she would be done for. Just one more! She was paralyzed with fear.

Randall, however, was elated.

"Woo hoo, Ruthy doooo! Told ya this was a good one."

The balance of the crowd did not share Randall's opinion.

"Awwww...it's too crowded up here already," grumbled Eamon. "Can't ya just let her go this time?"

"A pious woman would get this one easily," said the preacher.

"I know it," Agnes chimed in. "It's an easy one, for sure."

Constance was looking more satisfied every second.

"I like a good story before bedtime every night," she said, "That's how my other Mommy did it."

As cold as it was, Ruthy was sweating profusely. Morbid curiosity eeked it's way into her over-taxed brain. She focused on the one leg that remained against the far wall. Slowly, the toes on her dismembered leg began to wiggle.

"A letter then," Randall said firmly. "Let's have a letter."

Consciously, or no, he was rubbing his palms together again in anticipation.

Suddenly, there came a knock at the door.

CHAPTER TWENTY-FIVE

"How now, brown cow?" Randall shrieked, throwing up his hands as if he were annoyed. "I wonder who that could be?"

He looked as if he already knew though and his face remained gleeful as he hurried across the room to open the door. He did not seem surprised to see Grandma and the girls waiting on the other side.

"Yes, yes, do come in," he said and offered up a flourish. There were grunts and groans of displeasure from the crowd. "But hurry! Pick a side--any side--though in truth I fear that we're nearly done here."

Emma/Grandma entered first, followed timidly by Jenny and finally Dawny. Ruthy, who'd been praying fervently that someone would arrive in time, looked somewhat relieved.

"Grandma?" she pleaded. "Grandma, can you help me?"

There was momentary confusion on the old woman's face as Grandma Barnes stirred. She tilted her head briefly as though she were listening for a far off sound. Emma quickly regained control of Grandma and her face returned to normal. Emma was clearly afraid and Grandma's face said so.

Dawny, however, had been listening to the sounds of the game the entire way up the stair. While she in no way mistook Randall for a friend, she failed to grasp the serious nature of the thing and pushed around Emma to the forefront. She walked straight away to where

Randall stood and squared off, hands placed firmly on her hips.

"What the heck's goin' on in here, Mister? Why are you picking on Ruthy?" Her tone said that she certainly wasn't going to allow such a thing to continue.

"Oh ho!" Randall exclaimed. "I *like* this one! You're just full of piss and vinegar, ain't ya?"

Bending down, he tickled beneath her chin with his grimy pointer finger. Dawny shoved his hand away.

"I ain't messin' around with you, Mister. You let Ruthy go if you don't want some of this!" She held up her clenched fist to illustrate the point.

"Dawny, don't!" cried Ruthy. "Don't antagonize him."

Randall turned on Ruthy, his eyes narrowed.

"Antagonize? Antagonize, you say? That's a mighty big word for a girl who can't even get a simple puzzle right. I think I might have a lot more fun playing with your sister. At least she's not a fraidy cat."

Emma moved toward Dawny, in an effort to pull her back. But too late, as Ruthy's body slammed back into the shackles on the far wall and Dawny was hurled into the noose.

"Yikes!" Dawny cried. "Yikes, Mister, I was just kiddin' with ya. I didn't mean nothin' by it."

She looked more than frightened now. Jenny ran to the gallows and sat down next to Emma, taking hold of her hand.

"Don't worry, Dawny, we'll get you out of here," she said, "somehow."

"Let her go," Emma said. "You have no right—"

"None needed," Randall explained patiently. "Up here it's Randall's rules. Pick a side. Or did you want to join your little friend up front?"

Emma looked terribly uncertain now.

"Yeah, I thought so," Randall said. "You always were a little prissy, Emma Ten Broek, with your white lace and ribbons. Always were too goooood to play with the likes of me."

Emma gasped.

"Yeah, I knew it was you inside there," he continued. "You can fool some of the people, some of the time, but you could never fool an old fool like me."

Just then, the look of uncertainty changed into a look of ferocious determination as Grandma Barnes fought her way to the surface once again. She gave a mighty shove and her body contorted as she pushed an unsuspecting Emma to the side. Emma, once again in her own form, sprawled on the floor beside the old woman. Grandma Barnes was back and she was not happy. She began to advance on Randall, one, firm, Grandmotherly step at a time, and as she did so, she chanted.

"Yea, though I walk through the valley of death, I shall fear no evil."

Randall began to back away. His own face wore an expression of almost comical horror.

He'd had a grandmother too, once. The crowd watched in stunned silence as Grandma gained on him.

"For thine art with me," she continued. Thy rod and thy staff, they comfort me."

And then she was on him. With lightening quickness she reached out and snatched him by the ear, dragging him toward the door.

"Yea, though I walk through the valley of death," she repeated. "I shall fear NO evil..."

Randall wriggled and squirmed the entire way but try as he might, he could not escape her iron grip. Grandma Barnes and her God escorted Randall straight to the exit, and tossed him out the open doorway.

"Do not pass go," Grandma chuckled. "Do not collect two-hundred dollars!"

Randall ran.

Grandma turned on her heels and walked directly to the chalkboard. Picking up a piece of chalk, she sighed as she filled in the letters.

NO REST FOR THE

WICKED

"Honestly, Ruthy, you'd have had this one if you hadn't let your nerves get in the way."

Ruthy began to giggle. Randall's intended meaning had gone astray and the irony of the situation was not lost on her. Randall was running now.

Emma, who was still lying in a heap on the floor, just said, "Whoa..."

"Hmmmpffff," Grandma responded turning to face her, "Can't send a girl in to do a woman's work."

With that, she walked to the gallows and slid the noose from Dawny's neck. Dawny and Jenny began to climb down as Grandma addressed the others in the room.

"Well? What are you all waiting for? He has no hold on you. Never did, really. All you needed was a little faith."

She caught the surprised look on Preacher Tattersall's face.

"Well I'll be damned," the Preacher mumbled, shaking his head. "If you have but the faith of a mustard seed..."

"Hmmmppfff," she said again. "Shame on you, Preacher. Not much of a holy man, I'd say."

Emanuel Tattersall wasn't sure whether to be insulted or relieved.

"Go on then," Grandma said. "You're free now."

And indeed, the members of the ghostly congregation were beginning to rise and find their shackles gone. They began milling about, stretching their legs and rubbing their wrists and for a change, smiling.

"I believe Miss Emma can show you where to go next," Grandma continued.

All eyes turned to Emma as she gathered herself and rose to her feet.

"Yes, Ma'am, I sure can," she answered happily.

The spirits gathered round Emma and followed her out the door. It would be a full house at the council fire tonight. The girls ran to hug Grandma Barnes.

"Straight to your rooms now, and be quiet," she commanded. "Give your father a little time to cool off."

Ruthy promised that she'd do just that.

"Good," Grandma said. "I'm a little tired now. I'm going to sit for just a minute but I'll be down, by and by."

"Should we wait for you?" Ruthy asked.

"No need. I got up here on my own and I can sure enough get myself back down. You go on now and get yourselves to bed."

The girls turned toward the hallway and the middle room in which the passage to the cellar lie.

"And don't forget to say your prayers," Grandma called after them. Ruthy grinned. Grandma Barnes didn't change much.

And just like that the nightmare was over. Almost.

CHAPTER TWENTY-SIX

Grandma Barnes sighed as she watched the girls go through the doorway of the middle room of the attic. She'd done a good thing tonight. There was a time for anger and a time for forgiveness. Her grandchildren were fine people. They'd be all right if they'd only listen to what they were told.

Grandma, on the other hand, would not be all right. She was eighty-three years old and she was tired. But more than that, she was ready. She turned and walked back into the room. With a bit of manipulation she managed to lower herself to a sitting position next to the wall. And then she closed her eyes one last time and went to thank her God in person.

CHAPTER TWENTY-SEVEN

Immediately upon entering the middle room
of the attic, the three girls realized the
passageway to the cellar had gone. Of course!
That passage was a part of the past and as
such, it was tied to Emma. She was on her
way to the clearing now, the passage gone
with her. They dare not try the trap door to the
attic with Charles waiting just below. Dim light
flooded in from an outside lamp in the yard
beneath them.

"The roof!" Jenny said. "If we can get out there, we can drop down to Grandma's landing and go down the stairs."

She tried to slide the window up but many years of disuse had rendered it stuck.

"Help me push," she commanded.

"Look out, Pipsqueak," Ruthy said and Jenny moved to the side.

It took every bit of Ruthy's considerable strength to get the window sliding. The muscles in her biceps strained and her eyes bulged as she pushed with all she had. Finally, the window jerked and gave up a few scant inches. Ruthy shoved again and gained a few more inches. It was open by barely a foot when they heard their father shriek from down the hall.

"NOOOOOOOOOOOOOOOOOOOOOO!" Charles shrieked. And then, "MOMMMMMMAAA!"

Panic jolted through her like an electric shock. He was in the attic!

"Hurry, Ruthy!" Jenny cried.

She heard the first footfalls pounding down the hall towards them and realized with horror that they'd left the door standing wide open. He'd be on them in seconds.

Throwing her back into the task she shoved hard. The window gave up another six inches and jerked to a halt with a loud *thud*. A foot and a half of open space now stood between her and freedom. It wasn't much but it was all she was going to get. She grabbed Dawny first and shoved her out the window. Jenny was next. Ruthy was half way through the window herself when Charles stormed into the room. He spotted her right away and the look on his face was murderous.

"Sons-a-bitches!" he screamed. "You killed my mother!"

For a split second, Ruthy froze. What did he mean *killed* Grandma? They'd only just left her and she'd been fine. Grandma was...*dead*? *How*?

"When I get my hands on you, I'll kill you!" Charles screamed.

Ruthy was startled into action. He was half way across the room when she pushed the rest of the way out the window and made the roof outside.

Charles face was purple with rage.

It seemed as if he made the window in a single bound. He heaved on the thing throwing it wide. A quick leap and he was outside on the roof as well.

The peak of the roof was steep and the girls made their way toward the edge as quickly as they dare. Still, it was slow going and the landing seemed miles away. Ruthy gained the edge first and quickly dropped down onto the landing. She held her arms up and pleaded with the girls.

"Dawny, hurry!" she cried. "Jump."

But Charles Barnes was a man who just didn't give a damn anymore. He jumped the last few precarious feet and snatched Dawny up by the hair. Dawny howled as he dragged her back to the middle of the roof, the asphalt shingles tearing at her legs and ankles.

"Meany!" she yelled. "Owwwwyyyyy—it hurrrts!"

"Daddy, let her go!" Jenny cried, as she scrambled back towards her father and sister. "You're hurting her."

Charles let go of Dawny's hair, grabbing her left forearm instead.

"Yoo-hoo! Charles!" called a voice from below. Randall! He was giddy with excitement.

"I got this one, Brother," he went on. "Toss that little bag of turd down here. You'll want both of those arms free so you can send the next one down too!"

Completely overwhelmed by rage and grief, Charles never gave it a second thought. Jenny had just enough time to grab Dawny's hand one more time as Charles whirled around in a circle and flung both of them into the air like a shot-putt. She didn't even scream on their way down.

***

"When I pulled into the driveway just a moment later, Charles was dragging a hysterical Ruthy down the stairs by her hair. I could see Randall standing over the broken bodies of Jenny and Dawny in the yard below, though I did not know who he was at the time. He looked real enough though, just like you and me." Edward paused for a moment, choking on the words. Tears streamed from his faded, old eyes.

"'Bring that little bitch to me,' I heard him say as I jumped out of the truck and ran across the yard.

"I got there just in time to hear Jenny's last words."

"'Don't cry, Dawny,' she said, just like she always did. 'I got you.'

"She was still holding Dawny's hand, for Christ's sake! And then her own hand twitched for just a second and went still.

"'What the hell?' I started to holler but then I saw Annette pulling in.

"She slammed her car in park and jumped out. She didn't see Jenny and Dawny lying there. All she saw was Charles dragging Ruthy across the yard by the hair. And then she saw red.

"Charles froze and let go of Ruthy, staring at Annette now instead.

"'You Son-of-a-bitch!' she screamed, and made the side yard in what seemed like one superhuman leap. Diving at Charles, she raked her fingernails down both sides of his face leaving bloody trails behind.

"And then she started hitting him...she was beating the living hell out of him, punching him in the face and scratching the daylight out of him. He fought her right back but it was obvious he was losing this one. She fought like a wildcat.

"Me? I couldn't move. My mind couldn't begin to process all of this.

"Ruthy ran to where Jenny and Dawny lay. She knelt beside them, wiping dirt from their faces and brushing back their hair. Saddest thing I ever saw."

Eddy stopped talking. The muscles at the corners of his upturned lips tightened as he tried to regain control of his emotions. A moment later, he went on.

"And all the while, Randall just kind of hovered, with that stupid grin on his face, taking it all in. He babbled the entire time-- insane things--things that I can't remember now.

"Annette was hollering. Charles was hollering. The cows were hollering from the barn and ramming the doors and the walls.

"Ruthy was talking softly to the girls, but no matter what she said, Jenny and Dawny wouldn't say a word back to her.

"'They're mine now!' Randall cried, elated.

"Ruthy looked up at him and screamed, 'Leave them alone, you bastard! You can't have them!'

"At that moment, there was an audible *pop* and a dozen shadowy Indians stepped out from behind the trees. I was as stunned by this as anything else I'd seen that night. I'm telling you even the air changed at that moment. You could feel it! And I don't know what it was. All I can think of to call it is energy. But if it was energy, it was a lot of energy. The air kind of sizzled with it.

"Randall's whole attitude went from glee to fear and his jaw dropped as they circled round him. Annette stopped hitting Charles and we all just stood there in shocked silence. Even the warring cows seemed to have stopped, and the barn fell silent. The Natives left an opening

399

the width of two men on the far side of the circle; the side leading to the forest.

"Now this was the first I'd seen of those Indians. I realized immediately that they were no longer of this world. That much was easy to see. But what in God's name was going on? It was like my mind stepped out for a while and I couldn't think. Nor could I move. All I could do was watch, like I was at a show somewhere, instead of here on the farm...instead of here in my own body. Everyone else was frozen too.

"The masks of the False Face society were hideous enough on their own, carved to resemble horrible beings with swatches of course, black hair jutting out here and there. But even worse than that, I could see the whites of those Indian's eyes shining through the holes. And they all carried weapons. Some had hatchets. Others had clubs and spears. For a time, they stood stock still, just staring at Randall. And he never moved nor said a word. Scared too, I guess.

400

"And then one of the braves stepped forward, into the center of the ring. He began circling around Randall, loosely at first and slowly, coming just a bit closer to him each time. Randall turned with him in an effort keep him in his sight. When the brave was close enough to Randall that he could've smelled his breath, he stopped short. Leaning in, he stared straight into Randall's eyes, his hook nose nearly touching Randall's face. Time itself didn't even dare to pass while he stood there staring Randall down.

"All of a sudden, he let out a blood-curdling *whoop* that went right through me. Randall leaped for the hole in the circle and the sky was filled with war cries as the natives went after him.

"And it wasn't as though they were trying to catch him either. They were *herding* him! Having nowhere else to go, he ran straight for the woods. They'd catch up to his side, hitting him with a club or a tomahawk, and then fall

401

back a piece. I watched as they ran across the lawn and through the garden. A minute later they were all gone.

"When I looked back I saw Annette kneeling over the two girls. It was like she was trying to wake them up. She was patting their little faces, stroking their hair and pleading with them to come back.

"'Jenny? Baby? Wake up now, ya hear me?'

"I have no words to describe the desperation in her face at that moment.

"'Dawny? Please baby...wake up now for Mommy.'

"Three more figures stood now beside Annette and the girls. First, was the old Dowser, whom I recognized from that day in the cow pasture. With him, was another who was obviously a chief from the looks of his head-dress. The third one looked old and fragile and maybe even ill, and wore medicine bags around his neck and at his hip.

"The Dowser tipped his hat to me and said, 'Evenin', Edward.'

"'Who the hell—?' Charles began.

"'Shhh,' the Dowser said quietly, laying his pointer finger to his lips. And for some reason Charles stayed still.

"The Dowser turned back to me then.

"'I'm going to need you to keep an eye on this place for me,' he said. 'Don't let any more harm come to these children.'

"There was something strange about the look on his face. I felt like he knew something I didn't.

"'I can do that,' I said. I didn't know what else to say.

"Three more braves came from behind the trees leading horses. The Dowser and Chief Hadawa'ko carefully lifted Ongwaterohiathe onto the back of a beautiful paint horse. Hadawa'ko turned back around and looked at Annette. He didn't say a word but lay one hand over his heart, and held it there. Tears coursed down his cheeks. With a nod, he squatted down and put both arms underneath Dawny's body.

"'Wait! No,' Annette begged. 'Where are you taking my babies?'

"He didn't answer her but gazed steadfastly into her eyes as he lifted. His arms went right through Dawny's body and out the top, but rather than being empty, they cradled another translucent version of her body within. Gently, he handed this spiritual body up to Ongwaterohiathe, who laid it carefully over his lap.

"'Give her back,' Annette pleaded weakly, holding her arms up toward the medicine man. But you could see in her eyes that she knew the truth of it. She knew already that they weren't coming back this time.

"Hadawa'ko mounted his horse next and in much the same way the Dowser handed Jenny up to him. Finally, the Dowser climbed up on another horse, once again tipping his hat and the three just trotted away toward the garden, taking the spirits of Jenny and Dawny with them.

"Annette crumpled against the lifeless bodies of the children."

CHAPTER TWENTY-EIGHT

"And still, I could not move," Eddie went on. "I stood and watched as they went. They had no more than just got out of sight when the cows commenced to fighting again. Straight out of the blue we heard ranting and bellering and wood splintering. Likely they sensed those Indians had gone.

"The first of those cows, deep in the throes of madness, burst through the barn doors. Just one, at first, and she rammed through that wooden door like a bulldozer. Another came through right after, bellering to beat the band.

406

She quickly caught up to the first cow and began to systematically tear her apart, ramming and snorting, and even biting, though I'd never seen such behavior from a cow before. The noise was...horrible! All I could hear was hooves pounding and the *whump* of bone hitting meat as more and more of them got out.

"There must have been thirty or forty of the crazy buggers having it out right there in the front yard. And more were coming every minute!

"But Charles Barnes was not going to put up with that. He took one last look at Annette and walked with a purpose straight for the barn.

"'I'll deal with the lot of you when I get back,' he said looking directly at Ruthy. He didn't look none too happy when he said it but it was really the quiet, matter-of-fact tone in his voice that made my skin crawl. Veering to the left, he made a wide path around the fighting cows

407

and shortly thereafter made the milk house. Seconds later I heard that old bell ringing. He was calling the herd in just like it was time for milking.

"Every last one of those cows stopped dead in their tracks. One by one, they turned and made for the barn. One by one, they waddled that bag-too-full waddle back to where relief waited in the form of the automated milking system.

"And then I noticed Annette. She was still kneeling down by Jenny and Dawny, crying her eyes out. And then she looked up at me and in a split second the look in her eyes changed. It was as if something clicked in her mind and you could almost see in her eyes that she'd made a decision.

"'Get the girls in the house,' she ordered. 'Get 'em in where it's safe.'

"'What are you going to do?' I asked.

"'Right behind you, Eddie,' was what she said.

"Only she wasn't."

Chapter Twenty-Nine

The milking parlor was black as midnight when Annette pushed through the door. Fumbling for the light switch just inside, she found it already up and in the open position. *The cows must have knocked something loose and killed the power*, she thought.

She felt nothing, nor did she have any plan. What she experienced was more like a curious sense of tunnel vision coupled with complete and utter determination. She had made Charles a promise and she intended to keep it.

For right now, and for this moment, that was all that mattered.

A quick left turn and she was inside the closet-like space that served as an office. This wasn't the first time the barn had been without power. She reached for the oil lantern that they had kept on the desk and found it easily, a book of matches right beside it. As she lit the lantern, she could hear the restless shuffling of cows in the milking stations just inside.

"Charles?" she called. "Are you in here?"

There was no answer.

Lantern in hand, she left the office and turned the corner. Charles was nowhere in sight although he had managed to get the first set of six cows locked securely in their stanchions. These were quiet enough, busily grinding oats from their feed buckets.

The din from the barn was horrific though as the cattle out there fought to enter the holding area. A loud crash, the sound of wood splintering and a series of gut-wrenching snorts and bellers were followed by a string of expletives from Charles.

"Sons-a-bitches," he yelled. "Get back! I'll kill you, by the Jesus!"

Annette cocked her head and listened.

"MOTHER FUCKER!" Charles yelled, and then began to shriek with pain as the herd overtook him.

Annette smiled.

It wouldn't be hard to find him but she may want to hurry. She picked up her pace as she strode past the bulk tank and through the door to the barn. She could hear his cries for help coming from the far end of the barn. Fortunately, for her, he'd remembered to shut the gate from this end, leaving a clear path to the area in front of the mangers. This was a space roughly ten feet wide, isolated from the main floor by a series of upright poles, from which hired hands could throw hay and grain into the mangers at the fore of the stanchions.

"Help me," Charles moaned, "for the love of Christ, somebody—"

Annette marched towards the sound of his voice. She reached the far end of the barn just in time to watch a badly battered Charles crawl through the bars of a stanchion and into the safety of the feeding area. Relief flooded his face as he saw his wife just a few feet away.

"Annette! Thank God! Help me up, Honey," he pleaded from the floor. Blood flowed freely from his nose and mouth and one of his legs was obviously broken, judging by the way he dragged it all cock-noodled to the side.

"Does it hurt?" Annette asked him, a small smile playing at her lips.

Charles didn't seem to notice.

"Help me up," he croaked. "I need to go to the hospital. I hurt bad, Annette. I hurt all over."

"Good," she answered matter-of-factly, as she surveyed the loose hay on the floor around him.

"Huh?"

"You killed my babies," she said. "I told you what would happen…"

"Annette?" Fear clouded Charles' face as he realized that something wasn't right with her. The light from the lantern reflected a cool vagueness in her eyes. She looked…well, empty inside.

"Annette? Help me, Darlin', please," he pleaded.

Annette giggled.

"God-damnit!" Charles exploded, "Help me get the hell up and get out of here, you bitch! My fucking leg is killing me!"

Annette flinched. A look of confusion crossed her face. As she reached up to rub her forehead, she seemed to notice the lantern for the first time. The smile returned to her lips and she opened them as if to speak.

But the voice that came out of them did not belong to Annette. Nor did it belong to a woman. The distinctly male voice that came out of those lips, firmly but quietly, said only this:

"Burn in Hell, Charles Barnes, you Son-of-a-bitch!"

Annette tossed the lantern easily into a pile of hay.

Then she turned, and to Charles' horror, walked calmly in the opposite direction, back toward the milk-house.

And as she walked, she began to sing.

> 'Bringing in the sheaves,
> Bringing in the sheaves.
> We shall go rejoicing,
> Bringing in the sheaves...'

CHAPTER THIRTY

Eddie continued.

"At the end of the night, nary a cow remained living on the property. At the end of the night, the human body count was four. Charles' body was never found though and it was assumed he died in the fire. His mother, was also dead and by his own hand, his daughters, Jenny and Dawny. We all died a little that night—nothing was ever the same. I have sometimes wished that I had never turned the truck around. I have sometimes wished that on that hateful day, I had just kept on going.

"Five days later, at precisely 1:00 on a sunny summer afternoon, we buried nearly half of the Barnes family. I sat at Annette's right hand and listened to a pastor that had never met the first one of us, drone on about life and death and the mysterious ways of a God that I figured had never met any of us either. I was wrong.

"'Why does God take innocent children from their mothers,' he was saying.

"And I wanted the answer to that question. I raised my head and listened hard as I studied the bodies of Jenny and Dawny, all dressed in their Sunday best just to be laid in the dirty, cold ground. Like a million grieving mothers before her, Annette had chosen white dresses, all covered in lace, with which to bury her babies in. They should've worn those fancy dresses in their first school concert or to a friend's birthday party. Their hair, having been

417

brushed until it glistened, lay in deceptively lively curls around their still faces. It was all wrong. Gone were the sweaty cow-licks that she used to try and tame with spit and the palm of her hand. Gone were the plain brown, rubber-bands that they always wore to hold back their wild hair when they were playing.

"And I wondered *why? Why, if there was a God in Heaven, was a man able to throw his own babies off of a third-story roof? The same babies that hugged him and kissed him good night, wanting nothing more than to love him and be loved in return. Why?* I needed the answer to that question. Why *did* God take away these babies who'd had so little time on Earth to just run and play?

"The pastor had an answer for that. You'll want to take note of this, Father, because this was the only thing that comforted any of us at the time.

"'I've been asked this question more times than I'd like to remember,' he said. 'And

418

believe me, it took many years of prayer and questioning before I got that answer.'

"In all of my life, I had never been more in the moment as I was just then, straining to hear that answer.

"'And then one day, it came to me,' he said, 'and I knew. God does not take the little children from the breasts of their mothers. He does not cause the accidents, nor bring the illness that ends their lives so soon. God, in his infinite mercy, looks down upon us, and weeps as these tragedies unfold.'

"The preacher paused for a moment here, looking thoughtful, and then went on. 'No. He doesn't take your children from you. But he waits there, in his heaven. And if the worst should happen... If your child meets with an accident and dies... then he is there in Heaven to receive him.'

"I never heard another word he said that day. I was too busy weeping."

Indeed, tears now streamed down Father Murphy's face. He had no words. Eddie went on.

"I kept my word to the Chief. It took more than a year to rebuild the place. Adam came home from the hospital and moved into the house with us. The kid was like a son to me. He and Ruthy were allowed to date, while being chaperoned, of course, and he never left again.

"The picture in my mind? The one that kept turning to black and white? I never saw it again. I looked though, believe me. Constantly. Pretty near every time I headed out of the barn and for that house, I found myself staring, searching every inch of the place for any sign of color missing. And I figured as long as I didn't see that, then the place was doing okay.

"Soon after we got everything all fixed back up and squared away, I went looking for Annette. I found her sitting in that side porch again. She went there often, and for hours on end. I could see the tension in her body as she sat, leaning forward as though listening for something and all the while looking at that sidewalk which lay just outside the porch windows. She just sat there staring at the peeling paint of the hopscotch board on the cement. It was there that Jenny and Dawny whiled away many a summer's day.

"'Annette,' I said, getting down on one knee and taking her hands. 'I've loved you for as long as I can remember. There's never been anyone *but* you in my heart. If you'll agree to marry me, I promise I'll do anything and everything in my power to make sure that you and the kids never see another bad day in your whole lives. I'd like to take you away from here—away from the bad memories. I want to buy us a new house and start a brand new life.'

"She looked right through me. Didn't even seem to be considering, really. Just stared out at that sidewalk.

421

"Finally, after what seemed an eternity, she turned and looked straight at me.

"'Edward,' she said, 'as to your first question, I'd like to think on it a bit. But I think that sounds more than nice.'

"My heart soared.

"'As far as leaving here though,' she went on, 'it's out of the question. I've bonded to the place and I can't go now.'

"And then, just like clockwork, I heard the tinkle of laughter coming from the direction of the sidewalk. My head snapped up and around and I just caught the quick motion of a pebble flying lightly through the air. It landed just a few feet forward, on the number eight of that old hopscotch board.

"'Number eight!' Dawny's voice carried ever so lightly on the breeze. 'Number eight is good and great!'

"Then I heard Jenny giggle and the moment was gone.

"Annette just smiled and answered, 'Like I said, I've bonded.'"

The good Father smiled at this. A sense of peace and a good ending had come over him. Eddie, however, rubbed his head and stared intently at the bookcase to his left. After a moment, he turned back and faced the priest.

"We never spoke of that night again--ever. So you see, Father, between the things that I didn't do and should have, and the things that I did do and shouldn't have, I'm in a pretty big pickle here. And like I said, my time is short. A few days, maybe a week."

Father Murphy thought he knew just what to say now. He was relieved about that. He was also moved in a dozen other ways, but mostly relieved. And he was happy that the story was finally over.

"Eddy," he began, "Sometimes life is its own punishment. You've been through an awful lot. I have a feeling that God will be okay with you on this one."

He was prepared to go on if need be, but fully expected Eddy to rise, thank him profusely, and walk out the door--end of story. He was very pleased with himself.

"Well, I ain't complaining none," Eddy added, remaining firmly in his chair. "I've had a good life. The kids treated me like a real father and I appreciated that. It's been a pleasure and an honor to have finished raising them. And I've loved a good woman. I still miss Jenny and Dawny and wish to God I'd have done something for them. I hope and pray that God can forgive me for that one."

"He already has," answered the priest.

"But Father, there's more," Eddy went on. "When it's my turn, and that's gonna be real soon, I like to think I'll walk straight up to that portal, like a man and without fear, and pass through to the other side."

Eddie looked dubious.

"But?" questioned Father Murphy.

"But I can't help the thinking that when I get on the other side..."

Here he hesitated again, placing both hands over his face as if he could hide from the vision. He rubbed his face momentarily and when he removed his hands again, bright, new tears glistened in his frightened eyes.

"When I get to the other side," he continued, "I know that Charles will be waiting for me, and Charles Barnes is one, miserable Son-of-a-bitch when he ain't happy."

And in that cluttered, little office nestled deep inside the heart of a busy world, one could've heard a pin drop.

Sneak Preview!

Coming Soon...

Nathanial's Window: The Wrath of Jesse Eads

By

Peazy Monellon

Prologue: 1865

Jesse Eads read the truth in old Doc Baker's eyes the moment the old man stepped out of his son's bedchamber. Outside, the wind howled like a predator, blowing snow into head-high, icy drifts. He pulled his threadbare jacket closer and wrapped his arms round himself. He could no more quell his trembling than the worrisome wind.

He'd pretty much known the truth before Doc went in but there had been hope then.

"Are you sure, Doc? Nothing else you can do?" This last came out as barely a squeak and he realized he'd been holding his breath. He searched the doctor's face for any sign.

"I'm sorry, Jesse,' Doc answered, fidgeting with his battered, black hat. "The medicine's just not working."

"I see."

"I've made him as comfortable as I can," Doc Baker said. "Some laudanum to keep him quiet and help with the pain."

"Yes, comfortable," Jesse answered. "We should try to make him comfortable. Will you leave the bottle?" He was hard-pressed to hide the trembling now, though he tried.

"Of course I will. You might take a bit yourself. It'll help you rest."

Doc rooted in his worn, leather bag for a moment and produced a small glass bottle stoppered with a cork.

"Rest?" Confusion clouded Jesse's eyes. "Rest now? How long does he have?"

"Jesse," Doc answered weakly, "You have to take care of yourself—"

"I'll stay with him," Jesse said. He couldn't bring himself to say the words 'til the end'.

"Jesse—"

"Get the hell out of here," Jesse suggested. "Now." His voice was tight, his mouth dry. "Take the black and white pig on your way out. I reckon that will settle my debt."

Doc had been out here half a dozen times in a fort-night. Little Lucy had been the first to come down with Consumption. Baby Lucy lingered for days before she passed. He'd come twice more to see Jesse's wife, Caroline, who was half-mad with grief already and succumbed quickly. And now Nathanial.

Jesse stared straight ahead while the doctor gathered his belongings and saw himself to the front door.

Why? Why them and not me? Jesse wondered. They'd all had such high hopes when they'd rolled into town a year ago in a wagon piled high with their personal belongings, the milk cow tied to the back. Goshen was a new town, teeming with excitement--a fresh start. If he'd only stayed in Massachusetts they might still be alive now. If he hadn't been blinded by the chance to own more land, make more money... If only he could take all of this back, he'd give anything. Anything at all.

Alone again, he did the only thing he knew how to do at this point. He got down on his knees and prayed to Holy God above to spare his son. He prayed and he pleaded and he begged. He offered up himself and all his worldly goods. He repented every sinful thing he ever did and every errant thought he'd ever had. Jesse Eads prayed like there was no tomorrow. And the entire time he prayed, he knew that he was right about that. Tomorrow wasn't going to happen for Nathanial.

He never intended to go to sleep, but his God had other plans. Hours later, the fire mere embers now in the hearth, he awoke to the sound of his young son's raspy screams. Bolting upright, he realized he'd not been there to light the lantern. Nathanial had always been unbearably afraid of the dark.

"It's okay, Son," he shouted. "Papa's coming!"

"Papa?" Nathanial cried. "It's dark, Papa. I'm scared." His voice crackled like thin, dry paper as he struggled to push the sound out of his fever-burnt throat.

Jesse had been lying on the cold floor for a long time and as he rose, the muscles in his thigh seized up. He bit down hard on his upper lip and half dragged the useless leg across the floor. It took him only a moment to cross the room, his heart thundering in his chest, but that moment seemed to take forever. *How could he have forgotten*? *How could he have fallen asleep?*

He fumbled for the matches and the lantern on the chest beside the bed. And then he knew. The absence of sound roared through his head. Nathanial wasn't wheezing. His chest, which for days had labored intensely to draw minute breaths of air through heavy, fluid-soaked lungs, lay still. His eyes wide open, unshed tears puddling in them like dew on the windows of his newly-gone soul.

Jesse cried out in anger and frustration, cursing the god that had abandoned him.

Thirteen days later, Jesse buried his last reason for living. He'd special ordered the tomb from the stone-mason south of Goshen. It had cost him the cow and one of the horses from his team, but he didn't care. If that was the price for installing a glass pane into the rock casing, then so be it.

There was no funeral, no formal goodbye. Who'd have come? Consumption is contagious; far better to be alone in this. He knelt before his son's final resting place and made a solemn promise.

"You'll never have to be in the dark again, Son. Ever. You have my word on that." He'd have to trust to the moon and stars to help out in this, but the window would allow for some light at all times. Plus it was facing east, so every morning when the sun rose, it would shine for his Nathanial. He kissed his hand and lay his fingers against the thick glass. Then, sighing, he rose and mounted his horse.

Jesse Eads made one final stop on his way out of town. Reining his horse in, he dismounted and climbed the steps to the homestead. As he wandered from room to room (he was in no particular hurry—no place specific that he wanted to go), he straightened the bedclothes and opened all the curtains. Caroline would have liked that.

Dusk was fast approaching as Jesse lit the lantern in Nathanial's room. *Damn the darkness!* He dashed the lantern against the chest, breaking the glass, and tossed the flaming thing onto Nathanial's coverlet. Without prejudice, the hungry fire consumed both the bedding that Caroline had stitched by hand and the hateful sickness that had stole the reason behind it.

And then Jesse Eads walked calmly out of the house, mounted his horse and left town: no family, no wagon piled high, no cow tied behind. He'd lost everything, not the least of which was hope.

Nathanial's Window

CHAPTER ONE: 1977

Tommy Cooper had been in love with Beth Riley for as long as he could remember—at least since Beth's seventh birthday party when he'd accidentally hit her in the face with a snowball, knocking one of her molars out and making her cry. He owned those tears and he'd made a promise to himself right then and there that he was never, ever going to make her cry again.

And later, after he'd apologized for the millionth time, she'd forgiven him and presented him with the tooth, figuring he could use the tooth fairy money way more than she could. Besides, she added, the tooth had been loose anyways.

His pride was hurt a little bit. It was no secret that Mr. Riley was doing much better financially than Mr. Cooper who had problems keeping a job. The dining room table in the Riley house held a mountain of brightly-wrapped birthday gifts to prove it. The realization that Beth was aware of this disparity made him feel small.

But the tooth was a part of her and she'd given it to him. He'd taken it home later that day and wrapped it in a hanky, stowing it in his top dresser drawer. He carefully weighed the option of placing it under his pillow that evening and finding a dime underneath in the morning. There were lots of things he'd like to have and that dime would buy one of them. Ten pieces of penny candy--Mr. Adams, who owned the little market on the corner downtown, never charged tax when selling to children (as he said, 'The goddamned Great State of New York will get their hands on 'em soon enough').

Or maybe some bubblegum with a baseball card inside. Baseball was okay, he guessed, and he could sure use a few more cards to put in his bicycle spokes. His best friend Nicky Freeman had lots of them and they made the coolest sound when he rode by. But Beth had a way of making him laugh no matter how badly he felt sometimes.

In the end, he'd kept the tooth. And in the ten years that had passed since then, he hadn't regretted that decision even for a moment.

Beth was late today. They'd agreed to meet in the cemetery beside her house at four p.m. and he'd walked the two miles up the road in the August heat, arriving at what he figured was a few minutes early. That gave him just enough time to hide around the west side of the large sepulcher, mid-way through the grounds. From this vantage point he could peek through the shrubbery and around the corner, and get a clear view of the path beyond. This was a prank he pulled on Beth on a regular basis and he marveled at the fact that she fell for it every time.

The cemetery was Beth's habit, not his. He didn't understand her fascination with the dearly departed but that was Beth for you. That dark head of hers was filled with the craziest notions! He wasn't much of a believer himself, though here in the shadows, behind the cold, stone tomb, it was beginning to feel creepy.

No sooner did this thought enter his head when the nerve-endings on the back of his neck began to prickle. He suddenly *knew* he was being watched. Hot sweat turned icy cold on his back, and chill-bumps ran a marathon up his spine. Instinct told him to run but his legs disagreed, turning to jelly where he crouched. Whatever it was, it was watching him from behind. He could feel the sentient consciousness of it like a cool hand caressing his back.

Tommy listened hard, reaching for the hint of a sound from the tree-line thirty yards behind him. Somewhere off in the distance a gentle breeze kicked up the lonely tinkle of wind chimes. He was no longer sure from which direction the threat came and he searched the manicured lawn for any sign of movement. To his left, row upon row of neatly scribed, granite headstones. To his right, only the mottled gray stone of the crypt. Behind him—

Suddenly the air filled with the *whap-whap* of hundreds of wings as a flock of swallows took to the air, rocketing out of the trees.

"Gak!" he gasped, nearly wetting himself in the second it took for realization to set in. "Shit! You scared the hell outta me!"

Breathing again, he watched while the twittering birds made for the forest on the other side of the cemetery. And then chuckling to himself, he began walking back towards the path. He'd had enough of this scary crap for the day. He'd get Beth next time.

Huff came a noise… from behind him again. *Hhuff-huff!* It was the sound of ragged breathing—the breathless sound of something monstrously large and in charge running at top speed straight for him—something closing the distance fast.

Huff-huff, huff-huff, huff-huff…hufffff!

All reason left him as his legs took over and he ran. He felt the claws hit his back first and then fist-sized paws as he was knocked to the ground and pinned there. Every muscle in his body constricted at once, steeling him for whatever was to come.

"Topo!"

That was Beth's voice.

"Topo Gigio! Let him up!" She was laughing now, goddamnit!

"Gah!" he hollered, rolling over and pushing the rambunctious dog aside. "Only you would name a St. Bernard after a mouse!"

Topo crouched as if making ready to lunge again. His tail wagged wildly back and forth.

"Don't. You. Dare." Tommy said, pointing one thin finger at the amused animal. "Damnit, Beth, don't you own a leash, for God's sake?"

"Sit, Topo, sit." Beth commanded dropping lightly to the ground beside Tommy.

Topo responded by running excited circles around them, stopping to bark and pounce along the route.

They laughed about it later. That was after they'd torn off their jeans and tees and made love on the grass beside the swimming hole nearby. Topo belonged to Beth and that was good enough for Tommy. If she loved Topo Gigio, then he loved him too.

***

Tommy was in a high humor an hour later when he stepped into the kitchen at home, letting the screen door slam behind him.

"Whoa…that smells good! How ya feelin' today, Ma?"

It was good to see her up and around. Laura Cooper had recently been diagnosed with Lymphoma, a form of cancer of the lymphatic cells. And whatever that was (Tommy didn't understand all the medical mumbo-jumbo), it was aggressive. She was tired a lot now, and because of the chemotherapy, she spent long hours in her room, sicking up the chemical cocktail into a trash bin. Tommy stayed close to home those days, feeding her ice chips and dabbing her head with a cool cloth. She was growing thin and looked haggard, but today she was up and that was a good thing.

"Oh, I feel a lot better today. How was your day, Honey?"

Tommy immediately went to her and placed a gentle kiss on her cheek.

"Awww, c'mon, Tommy. Give your momma a hug. You're not gonna break me, ya know."

Laughing, Tommy picked her up and spun her around. Her arms around his neck felt good—felt like home.

"You're getting fat, Ma," he joked. "Must be all those ice chips I've been feedin' ya."

If Beth was the love of Tommy's life, Laura Cooper was the light. Besides, the kitchen smelled like ham and that was his favorite. His mother had a way in the kitchen.

Too late, he noticed John Cooper standing in the doorway, glaring, the requisite can of Miller in his hand.

"Where ya been, boy? I coulda used your help in the shop today."

John wasn't Tommy's biological father. His real father had been killed in a car accident when he was just a baby. He had only the vaguest memory of a fair-haired man with laughing eyes presenting his mother with a gift the Christmas before the accident. Laura had looked happy then, but her name had been Siefert, not Cooper.

John Cooper had arrived on the scene roughly three years later and had adopted Tommy in an effort to erase the past. Genetics will out though, and Tommy's long, blonde, curly hair and blue eyes were a daily reminder and a stark contrast to John's own dark hair and brown eyes.

Lately, John had been doing mechanical work out of his garage. Nothing major, really, just simple things like changing the oil and tuning up engines. He hadn't the equipment to do the big stuff. And since most of the men in town did these things for themselves his clients were limited to the big wigs, bankers and insurance salesman and such, who had no mechanical ability whatsoever and only came to him because he was a good bit less expensive than Smith's Garage on Riverview. John generally thought of them as idiots ('any man who can't change his own god-damned oil...') but then again, these were the same men who wouldn't think of inviting John Cooper to play in their golf league or attend their secretive meetings down at the Mason's lodge.

Tommy dreamed of becoming a musician. He'd been saving up for a guitar and planned on teaching himself to play as soon as he had enough money. His father had other plans for him. He insisted that one day Tommy would take over the business and toward that end he'd been teaching him. But no matter how well Tommy thought he was doing, the look on his adoptive father's face said the same old thing—*you didn't do enough, Tommy, didn't do it right, didn't do it when I said I wanted it done.*

"I'm sorry, Dad. I'll stay home tomorrow and finish up Mr. Clark's Chevy--"

John Cooper cut him off with a grunt. He was a man of few words, and the grunt covered a whole lot of them. Mostly, Tommy didn't want to hear them anyway. Gently, he set his mother back on her feet.

"Why don't you go wash up for dinner, Tommy? You can work all this out later," Laura said, smoothing her simple housedress.

She was wearing that nervous smile now—the one that made her look older and well...smaller somehow. Tommy took her cue and attempted to squeeze through the kitchen doorway past his father who wasn't budging.

"Excuse me?"

Another grunt. As their eyes locked, Tommy turned sideways and squeezed through anyway though John Cooper made sure that their shoulders bumped along the way.

Minutes later the Cooper family had gathered around the table. The clock on the wall said 6:15, but of course it was set to fifteen minutes fast. Dinner was at six o'clock sharp in the Cooper household. Six o'clock, not six-ten or six-fifteen. The ticking of the clock was the loudest sound in the room as John Cooper carved the ham. *'Time is money,'* it said.

"As long as you're feeling better tonight, I'm going to need you to write out some bills, Laura," John said, spearing a slice of ham and passing the platter. "We got doctor bills piling up."

"I'll get to it right after dinner," she replied, passing the ham to Tommy's half-sister Julie, who was thirteen. Julie had the proper color hair and eyes--dark, like John's.

"You're not eating?" John said, noticing that Laura hadn't taken any ham.

"I'll have a little something. Maybe just some bread and butter. I'm not real hungry tonight."

Another grunt. This one said that maybe if she'd eat, she'd get well and stop causing all this trouble. Tommy had the ham now and helped himself to a slice.

"Bob Jackson must owe me pretty near fifty bucks by now."

The mashed potatoes made the rounds next. *'Tick-tock,'* the clock said—*'times a wastin'!'* John made to spoon the peas onto his plate. A look of disgust passed over his face as he glared into the bowl and then turned those steely eyes toward his wife.

"Christ, Laura! There's hair in the peas! Now how am I supposed to eat that?"

Laura hadn't time to answer him yet when he reached over and gave a quick tug on her short hair, coming away with an entire lock of the stuff. He looked as though *he* was going to be ill now and that didn't make him happy at all. No one moved. No one breathed.

Grimacing, John Cooper tossed the lock of hair to the floor.

"Christ," he repeated. "Now your hair's falling out."

Laura slid back her chair and made to get up.

"I'll make some more," she said, her cheeks red with embarrassment. "It'll just take a few minutes."

"Pass the peas," Tommy said. His voice was tight, his blue eyes locked on John's brown ones.

"Well, you'll have to wait now, won't you?" John answered coolly.

"Pass me the goddamned peas!"

Tommy didn't wait for John to pass the bowl, but instead reached over and took it. He piled an extra scoop on his plate making sure he got the peas with the hair in them. That was his mother's hair and he'd take it. He began shoveling peas, hair and all, into his mouth, glaring back at John as he swallowed. If Laura Cooper had anyplace to run to, she'd probably have run then. Instead she sat back down.

John Cooper took another swig of his beer and grunted. *You make me sick, Tommy, with your wrong-colored hair and eyes. You make me god-awful sick!*

They finished the meal in silence while the damnable clock ticked on.

Scheduled to be released through Amazon in 2012.